CLAIMING ELLIE

STEPHANIE JULIAN

MOONLIT NIGHT PUBLISHING

She has one wicked desire…

Elise Perrault has more money than she could ever spend in a lifetime, but it can't buy her happiness. Or a lover. She wants a man who sees her as a woman and not a wealthy heiress. She wants a steamy affair with a hot guy to fill the ache inside her. Her dating drought has lasted more than a year so she creates a fake profile to find a no-string-attached lover. But two of her sexiest staffers discover her plan and plot to come to her rescue.

They'll make her wish come true…

Hard-ass Manny Bianchi and playboy Rob Henry have been friends since boarding school and work together at Perrault Financial. Manny, chief security officer, believes he and Rob can safely give Elise what she wants. Rob, bored with his job, is always looking for the next thrill. Rob knows Manny's been lusting after Elise for years. So has he, but he never wanted to cross that line. Until now.

Can Manny and Rob turn Elise's bad decision into the best decision of their lives? And can a no-strings-attached romp become lifelong love?

ONE

"Good morning, Miss Perrault. How are you today?"

Ellie Perrault caught herself before she tripped over her own feet at the sound of that smooth, deep voice coming from behind her.

Damn, damn, damn.

She hadn't expected to find anyone in the executive halls of Perrault Financial this early in the morning. It was just before eight, and she'd wanted to talk to her godfather before his day got out of hand. Jack's days were always out of hand by ten.

She needed to be at the arts center by nine and downtown Philadelphia traffic was horrendous on a good day. And, if she were honest, she'd wanted to avoid running into *him*.

How embarrassing would it be to literally fall at this man's feet? How did he do this to her every time? She didn't even like Rob Henry, so how did he manage to make her feel like a gawky twelve-year-old?

Drawing in a breath, Ellie forced a smile and turned to face the one person she'd been hoping to avoid.

Only to realize he wasn't alone. Of course, he was with the

only man she wouldn't mind seeing a lot more of. And who barely noticed her.

"Good morning, Mr. Henry." She nodded and tried not to look like a deer in the headlights. "Mr. Bianchi. I'm fine, thank you. How are you both?"

Rob smiled and, damn him, she felt a little flutter low in her gut. Women had been known to throw their panties at him. And if the guy hadn't been a stunted man-child with an ego the size of Manhattan, she might've been among them.

Liar. There's no might've about it.

Movie-star handsome, Rob came by those looks honestly. As in, his dad was an actual movie star. Rob's golden-brown hair had auburn highlights and was just a little too long to be considered clean-cut. His eyes were so blue most people thought he wore contacts. He didn't. He had a square jaw and cheekbones to die for. His eyelashes had their own damn Instagram hashtag, for heaven's sake.

And there was no way she was going to think about the recent spread in *People* magazine, the one where he was half naked in almost every picture. Sue her. She'd looked.

And the man had brains to go with those looks. He was only thirty-one and already chief operating officer of Perrault Financial. You didn't get to the highest ranks of one of the country's leading financial firms without serious smarts. Too bad he knew just how handsome and just how smart he was.

The man standing beside him was his opposite in every way. Perrault's chief security officer was quiet. Some might say to a fault. But Manny Bianchi would never fade into any background.

Dark brown eyes so intense that when he looked at her, she tingled in places she couldn't mention in public. Hair so dark it had blue highlights in the sun. His face wouldn't look out of place in an Italian museum full of Botticellis and Rembrandts.

And though she'd never seen Manny's body half naked and on glossy magazine pages, damn it, she was pretty damn sure he was just as hard and ripped as Rob.

She'd absolutely be willing to take one for the team and compare the two.

Of course, that would never happen because she would never get her hands on either body. Neither man had ever looked at her like they wanted to devour her. And she'd decided she was never again going to settle for a man who didn't want to tear her clothes off in lust.

That's what you get for dating a guy who promised you great sex then told you it was your fault he couldn't make you come.

"Everything's just fine, Ms. Perrault. Thank you for asking."

The hint of humor in Rob's voice made her back teeth grind. She swore he took way too much enjoyment in yanking her chain. She had no idea why. She'd never once said anything mean or nasty about him, at least not to his face or out loud to anyone, even though she did think he was an overbearing, egotistical—

"Is Jack in his office?" Manny disrupted her thoughts, as he managed to do every time she was with him. "He wanted to talk to us."

Ellie's thighs clenched at the combination of his voice and his gaze leveled directly at her. God, she hoped she didn't drool. Rob would love nothing more than to laugh at her while she drooled over Manny, who'd never seen her as anything other than the "Perrault Heiress." Or, even worse, as the dumb blonde who needed to be saved from the gold-digging boyfriend.

Rob just thought she was a cold bitch. Which was fine. She didn't care what he thought. Much.

Not at all.

Yeah, right.

She gave her head a little shake then realized they probably thought she was answering his question. *Ugh.*

"He is." She forced a smile. "Go ahead in. Have a nice day."

"You do the same, Ms. Perrault."

Her attention turned to Rob again and the smile that made butterflies explode in her gut. Why did he do this to her? She didn't even like him.

Why do you let him?

Very, *very* good question.

Her attention turned once again to Manny, who nodded, looking like he'd already dismissed her.

And why did the simple act of Manny staring at her make her want to rip off his clothes and shove him up against a wall so she could kiss him? And why did every little thing Rob do make her want to smack him? And then run her hands all over his body. Then maybe smack him again.

She dismantled a sigh in mid formation. She needed to find a man to work out this sexual frustration. And she needed to do it soon.

"Well. I'll see you...later."

She actually lifted her hand to wiggle her fingers at them before she turned and made a beeline for the elevator at the end of the hall.

Was it bad that she hoped they were watching her ass?

She definitely needed to get laid.

"ROB, Manny. Come in. Sit down. Shut the door."

Well, shit. Any conversation that started like that was not one Rob wanted to have. Especially not with his boss.

He and Manny had walked through the front door of Perrault Financial ten minutes ago. They'd taken the elevator to the top floor and headed for their offices, across the hall from one another.

Rob had fired up his computer, taken off his coat...and the second his ass had touched his desk chair, his office phone had buzzed. Jack's name had popped up on the screen, and Rob had bitten back a curse. There were only two things Jack ever called him into his office for on a Monday morning—a potential problem or an actual disaster.

Since Rob hadn't caught even a whiff of potential disaster online or on the morning news, and it was his job as Perrault's COO to know about this shit before the CEO of the entire fucking company, he could only assume this meeting was about him.

And yeah, maybe there might've been potential for personal disaster over the weekend, but he'd handled it. Like he always did. The fact that Jack might've caught wind of it was cause for concern, however.

When he'd stepped into the hall on his way to Jack's office, Manny had been there.

"He called you, too?"

Manny had nodded. "Yep. Think he found out about your near-death experience?"

Fucking Manny. Always the fatalist. Of course, Manny's childhood hadn't exactly given the guy a rosy worldview.

"I wasn't anywhere close to death."

Manny had stared at him. "Your parachute malfunctioned. The only reason you're not dead is because you learned your lesson the last time and had a backup. And you knew it was dangerous or you would've told me where you were going this weekend."

Busted.

He'd still been trying to think of something, anything to say to Manny, when the one woman in the world immune to his charms—and the one woman he seriously wanted to fuck and couldn't—left Jack's office.

Gonna be one of those days.

And now…this.

"What can we do for you, Jack?"

He wanted to add that he had a meeting in thirty minutes with the heads of the European divisions , but he suspected Jack knew that. Which meant Jack held a tactical advantage. The fact that the guy was his boss should've meant Jack always held a tactical advantage.

Better keep that in mind.

Tall, broad, and bald, Jack Octavian leaned back in his chair, looking like he'd stepped off the football field after his team had lost a big game. "You can tell me why you decided to jump off a mountain. That would be a good start."

Shit. This was exactly what he hadn't wanted to hear this morning. But it was his own damn fault. Fun always came with a price. He should know that by now.

"The mountain was there. I had a parachute. I landed. No problem."

Out of the corner of his eye, he saw Manny's jaw clench so hard, the muscles jumped under the skin. Goddamn, he hated when Manny was right. At least about bad news. And Manny was almost always right.

Rob shrugged, as if there'd been absolutely no risk, when that wasn't exactly the truth. Of course there'd been risk. There'd been a hell of a lot of risk, which was why he'd done it. Actually, it was the *only* reason he'd done it.

Jack didn't actually sigh, but he certainly looked like he wanted to. In fact, Rob was pretty sure his boss was pissed. Which made sense, considering he'd promised Jack he wouldn't jump out of or off of anything higher than a ladder after his last adventure had ended with a compound fracture of his left leg.

"Seriously, Jack, it wasn't a big deal. Whoever told you about my excursion exaggerated the danger."

And he wondered who that had been. Beside the other people on the plane, the only person he'd told about his outing was Manny. Manny had his back. Manny might not agree with all his life choices, but he was the one person Rob knew would always stand by his side. Always.

"A photographer on your flight recognized you." Jack's expression darkened even more. "Not exactly hard to do. Made a fair amount of money from a couple of tabloids before I shut him down."

"Are the pictures good?"

Jack's cheeks flushed brick red against his dark skin.

Shit. Probably shouldn't push the guy any farther than he already had. Rob held up his hand before Jack or Manny could blast him.

"Sorry. I'm sorry. I know we agreed I'd be more circumspect with my extracurricular activities. This was a once-and-done. A split-second decision. Won't happen again."

Because COOs of multinational, billion-dollar companies in charge of rich people's money didn't throw themselves out of airplanes or off mountains. At least, they didn't do it where the paparazzi could get photos of them. That was reckless.

And COOs weren't supposed to be reckless. They were stable. Sedate. Trustworthy. None of which applied to Rob. Which, to be fair, Jack had known when he'd hired him. So none of this was a surprise. Maybe the only surprise should be that it'd taken Rob jumping off a mountain with a parachute to finally push Jack to confront him. His boss hadn't said anything about the cliff diving in Kaunolu in December or the free climb in Arizona last summer.

Of course, Jack probably didn't know about those. Rob planned to keep it that way. And he hadn't been kidding about it not happening again. He'd nearly killed himself on the landing Saturday. He'd need a hell of a lot more practice if he went parajumping again.

But there was always another adventure out there. Another mountain to climb, a river to raft. A woman to seduce.

With the exception of one.

Jack shook his head, pulling Rob's attention away from the one woman he shouldn't want and couldn't have. Rubbing a hand over his shiny pate, Jack looked enough like Sarge from *Aliens* that all he needed was a cigar and an Uzi.

"Goddammit, you're gonna get yourself killed. And then I'm gonna kill you myself."

Stifling a laugh at the ridiculousness of that statement, Rob nodded, trying like hell to look sufficiently chastised. But he couldn't help himself. His lips twitched into a grin.

With a sigh, Jack shook his head. "Christ, I'm not trying to tell you how to live your life. That's not what this is. This is me telling you people are watching. Important people. People who make decisions about their money based on how much they trust the man in charge of it. If they think you don't care enough about yourself, they're not going to trust you with their money. And that's a bad thing for the COO of a financial company.

"Look," Jack included both him and Manny now, his gaze bouncing between them, "I don't expect him," he pointed at Manny, "to be your keeper. But no one is irreplaceable, and one of these days, you're not going to be able to flash a smile and talk your way out of losing your job. Or you're going to fucking kill yourself by jumping off a goddamn mountain because it was there."

Rob wiped any hint of a smile off his lips, realizing Jack wasn't just pissed. Rob had scared him. And that was worse. Because Rob respected Jack. And Jack cared what happened to him.

They'd had had this conversation before, about a year ago, the first time a client had mentioned seeing Rob on the pages of a tabloid skiing down a Swiss mountain in front of an avalanche.

In his defense, he hadn't planned to outrun an avalanche. And it was a hell of a photo. He'd bought a copy to hang on the wall of his apartment. But he'd never expected the photographer to sell it to a leading outdoor magazine. He'd also never expected a reporter to follow up with an interview request. He hadn't thought twice about it until a photo of him shirtless and smiling on a surfboard in the same article went viral. Then Jack had called him into his office to say Perrault's wealthiest client had asked if their COO planned to grow up before he jumped out of a plane without a parachute because he thought it made him look cool. Rob had had a smart-ass comment on the tip of his tongue but swallowed it when he'd realized Jack hadn't been smiling.

"I understand." And he did. He wasn't stupid.

Jack nodded. "I hope you do. Because I'd hate to see you blow your whole damn career out of the water for a reckless thrill. I also know you'll continue to do what you want because it's who you are. It's what makes you damn good at your job. But you're going to need to make some hard choices soon. If you don't, those decisions may be out of your hands."

"WELL, that went better than I expected."

Manny clenched his jaw shut at Rob's statement, trying not to say anything he'd regret later. Because Rob wasn't just a colleague. Manny considered him his brother and trusted the guy with his life, as long as Rob didn't make him bungee jump off an abandoned bridge or raft down an uncharted river. But as chief security officer for Perrault Financial, it was Manny's job to be in the damn boat, protecting Rob's ass from his seriously questionable choices.

Because that's what Manny did. He made sure Perrault and its assets were safe, whether from physical harm or cyberattack. As one of the few companies in the world that provided funds for high-risk, high-reward ventures, Manny made sure the money men, like Rob, made it home safe at the end of the day, whether they were in a Venezuelan jungle or on Wall Street.

His stint in the army after high school had honed skills he'd learned on the streets at an early age. And when he'd decided he'd had enough after six years and needed a change before he did something crazy, like reup for another tour in special ops, Rob had dangled this job in front of him.

And because Manny trusted Rob, he'd made the jump from military to corporate. And found an entirely different jungle to navigate. One he usually enjoyed. Rob knew him well.

"You talk to your dad recently?" Manny knew Rob just as well.

Rob paused for a second. "You're a son of a bitch."

"I'll take that as a yes."

Reaching his office, at the opposite end of the building from Jack's, Manny opened the door and walked through. Rob followed, like he knew he would.

"Not everything has to do with my dad. Or your mom, for that matter."

Manny dropped into the chair behind his desk, breathed out a sigh and leaned back as far as he could go.

"True. But my mom's gone and your dad's still around fucking with your head."

Rob sank into the chair across from Manny, shaking his head. "You're a pain in my ass."

"Also true. I'm also trying to save your ass from being fired."

"Fuck." Frustration hardened Rob's face, an expression few

people outside their small group of friends ever saw. "I don't know why I even take his fucking calls anymore. I know they're just going to piss me off."

"What'd your dad want this time?"

"What I don't want to give him. My time." He sighed. "A photo op of the Phillips family, the average family who happen to be Hollywood Royalty. But it wasn't for my dad. It was for my mom."

"So she's still threatening to run for governor?"

Rob snorted, shaking his head. "Yeah. Except now I think it's really happening. He called to trot us out like we're the fucking Brady Bunch. And he knew I wouldn't turn him down because it's for my mom."

"What does Safi say?"

"You know my sister. Anything for family."

And Manny knew Rob. "When's the shoot?"

Rob grimaced. "Next week. I have to be in Virginia Tuesday."

Manny grinned. Rob shot him the finger.

"So...what? You were hoping you'd break another leg and wouldn't be able to participate?"

Manny leaned back in his chair, watching Rob flounder. In public, the guy never lost his cool. He made everything look easy. It'd be easy to hate him if you didn't know him. If you didn't know that behind that easygoing front was a man who adored his mom and sister and had a difficult relationship with his dad that could fuel a blockbuster film.

He'd do anything for his friends, but he didn't have a lot of them. That didn't mean he wasn't friendly. A lot of people mistakenly thought they knew him. Most of them didn't.

Rob shook his head. "Damn, why didn't I think of that?" Then he sighed. "No, I just... I've been thinking that maybe...it's time for me to do something else."

Manny nodded, knowing Rob was watching his response like a hawk. Manny had known this was coming. Rob had been unhappy for a while. Selfishly, Manny hadn't wanted to push the subject. But he wouldn't be much of a friend if he didn't want Rob to be happy.

"Have you thought about what that might be?"

Rob shook his head. "It's just... I've been more restless than usual and that's not good. Not for me. Or anyone else around me. It's not fair to you or Jack or anyone we work with if I'm not a hundred percent committed. Christ, Manny, I'm fucking bored."

And for Rob, that was more dangerous than jumping off any damn mountain.

"You could've seriously fucked yourself up this time."

Rob shrugged. "I didn't. Moot point."

"No, it's not. Goddammit, Rob—"

"When are you gonna ask her out?"

The complete one-eighty made Manny's head spin, but he'd known Rob a long time. He knew his friend's moods and his tactics. He also knew Rob was fighting inner demons Manny couldn't battle for him. So he let him change the subject.

"What the hell are you talking about?"

Rob's smile spread slowly, all trace of his previous mood gone. For now. "The way she looks at you... You're an idiot if you don't take her up on that."

Yeah, he was an idiot. But not for the reasons Rob thought. No, he was an idiot because he'd been thinking the same thing. But Ellie was out of his league. Not because she was one of the richest women in the States, but because she was too damn sweet. Too fucking *nice*.

And he most definitely wasn't.

"She doesn't know me. And if she did, she wouldn't want me."

"Bullshit." Rob's voice had hardened, a tone not many people heard from him. "You're not your parents. Someday, you need to start believing that."

Manny took the opening Rob had inadvertently given him. "Neither are you. When are *you* going to figure that out?"

TWO

"What would you say if I asked you to help me set up a fake profile so I can meet a guy who has no idea who I am and have a one-night stand?"

Four faces with expressions ranging from "OMG, did she just say that?" to "WTF, I can't believe she just said that" stared back at her.

When not one of them spoke up after a few seconds, Ellie had to stifle the urge to beg her friends for help. It'd taken her two weeks to work out exactly how to phrase her plan, but now she wondered if she'd screwed up the reveal. Still, she wasn't going to back down now. For two weeks, she'd thought through all the angles, weighed the pros and cons, and finally decided this was the best course of action to cure her problem.

After all, she hadn't been on a date or had sex in almost a year, not since the Trent fiasco, and, damn it, she was lonely. And more than a little horny. And she wasn't about to apologize for that.

However, she did need help implementing her plan, and that's where her friends came in. Friends who were obviously dumbfounded by her brilliance, if their continued silence was any indication.

"Oh, come on." Ellie waved a hand in the air, as if she could magically make them talk. "I can't believe none of you have ever considered it. I mean," she swept a hand in Whitney Snowden's direction, "not you. You've got two men ready to do your bidding. When one's tired, I'm sure the other is ready and willing to fulfill all your desires. But the rest of us have to rely on battery operated boyfriends, and I, for one, am sick and tired of it."

It took a second, but, finally, Whitney burst into laughter, covering her mouth with one hand as she tried not to snort. Brianna Larose and Bailey Jolie exchanged a look, their brows rising practically to their hairline, while Marielle Aegeus shook her head, eyes wide.

"Seriously, guys," Ellie huffed. "I'm counting on you to help me."

Because she didn't think she could pull this off without help. Or encouragement. And maybe one foot on her butt pushing her out the door.

Ellie considered herself a smart person. She ran a respected nationwide charity, for heaven's sake. She could organize a five-thousand-dollar-a-plate event for five hundred people and deal with a fire in the caterers' kitchen hours before butts hit the seats. She could coordinate thousands of wishes made by termi-nally ill children through the Perrault Family Charitable Foundation and have time to volunteer at the Perrault Center for the Arts in downtown Philadelphia, where she taught after-school classes to underprivileged children, ranging from piano lessons for five-year-olds to vocal coaching for teenagers from local high schools whose music departments had been gutted.

None of that left a lot of time for socializing, but when she had a night to herself, she wanted to blow off steam. In bed.

With a guy. A decent guy who was after her for her body, not her money. But to pull off her plan, she needed the help of the women she considered her closest friends.

Whitney finally lost the battle against snorting, while Bailey shook her head and leaned forward.

"Normally, I'd be the one telling you to go for what you want." Bailey's expression screwed up into a frown. "But...a dating app? I don't know. I mean, I'm sure there're a *few* decent guys on them, but... What if word gets out that one of the richest women in the country is looking for some random guy to swipe right? You're either going to break the app or wind up on the front page of the *New York Times* as a cautionary tale."

"Which is why," Ellie practically bounced in her chair, excited to share her amazingly brilliant plan, "I want you all to help me create a fake profile. So I can find someone who won't know who I am. At least not right away."

Her friends glanced at each other as they sat, wineglasses in hand, around the huge sectional in Ellie's Philadelphia apartment that she shared with Bailey. Brianna and Mari had recently moved into Whitney's former apartment across the hall after Whitney had moved in with Chase and Ryan across town a couple of months ago. Whitney had hit the jackpot and found two men who loved her and didn't mind sharing her. Sure, she'd married one of them to secure her inheritance, but that didn't mean they weren't all going to live happily ever after.

Not that Ellie wanted happily ever after. Right now, she'd settle for happily-got-laid. She'd been on a really long dry spell. Way too long.

Bailey looked back at her with a glint in her eyes that made Ellie grin. When Bailey got that look, wonderful things happened. Or she made things go boom. Her dad was an inventor and allowed her free rein in a laboratory stocked with explosives. But Bailey was a curator of antique books at the Free Library of Philadelphia and not a trained scientist so...

"Fake profile, huh?"

Ellie's grin widened.

"Yes." She leaned forward, speaking directly to Bailey now. "All we need to do is find a stock photo that kinda looks like me, doctor it up a little and create a profile. It can't be that difficult. I mean, I'm sure serial killers do it all the time looking for victims and they don't get caught until after."

"Uh..." Brianna's eyes widened so far Ellie worried it had to hurt. Mari and Whitney looked at her with almost identical, open-mouth shock on their faces. Ellie would've laughed if she hadn't been so damn serious. "Maybe we shouldn't choose the app that has the serial killers."

Bailey's droll-humored statement broke the ice, and her friends started to talk over one another.

"Do you really think a fake photo will work?" Whitney seemed to be considering the possibilities. "I do have a little experience with Photoshop..."

"Don't they check your background before they allow you to use their site?" Brianna just looked confused. "Do you think that's how the serial killers get on?"

"Oh, this is going to be fun." Mari clapped her hands together, her expression gleeful. "Let me get my laptop."

TWO HOURS LATER, three laptops sat open on the dining table, littered with four empty wine bottles, two crumpled bags of Doritos, and three—why were there three?—enormous, almost-empty bags of Peanut M&Ms.

Mari had found a stock photo they all agreed kind of looked like Ellie but not enough that anyone would think, "That's heiress Elise Perrault." Whitney had used Photoshop to darken the model's hair just enough that it definitely did *not* resemble Ellie's dark-gold color at all. The model's hairstyle was different, as well, and when Whitney was finished tweaking the model's nose and the background of the photo, they all agreed this might actually work.

They'd also agreed she should be an elementary school-teacher, which would explain the lack of social media, and they chose a name that was common enough so if someone actually went searching for her online, there were hundreds of people with the same name in the same age group. It would take hours to search through them all.

"So," Mari took a swig of wine before shoving her glass across the table for Bree to refill, "are you ready to kick this pig?"

Feeling no pain after two or three (okay, maybe four) glasses of wine, Ellie's nose wrinkled. "I would never do that. Why would anyone want to kick a pig? What did the pig do to them? Isn't that animal cruelty?"

"Of course it is." Bailey sniffed. "Unless the pig's a man. Then it's perfectly okay."

With a shrug, because she really was feeling no pain, Ellie turned Mari's laptop toward her. They'd filled out the entire profile on the second most-popular dating website in the country. All that was left to do was press the button and she, or rather, Tiffany Adams would be available to be hit on by thousands of men.

When she thought about it like that, doubt started to creep in. What if no one wanted to date her? What if they looked right over her picture? What if...

Ellie looked around the table at the other women.

"You guys won't let me make a fool of myself, will you?"

Bailey snorted and rolled her eyes, but Whitney cut in before Bailey could speak.

"You know you don't have to do this, right?" Whitney reached across the table to grab Ellie's hand. "I'm just saying, I can ask Chase or Ryan to set you up with someone. They know lots of guys."

Ellie shook her head. Chase and Ryan were good friends with Manny and Rob. She *so* didn't want them knowing she was having trouble finding dates.

"We know all the same people. I don't want to screw around with someone I'll have to see at every function I attend from now until eternity." Like Trent. Damn him. She'd made that mistake once and was still paying for it. Luckily, her former boyfriend had unexpectedly moved to Europe. Good riddance. "I want to be nobody for a couple of hours. I need to date someone who doesn't know who I am or how much I'm worth. Someone who isn't calculating how much they could get in a divorce from our first date. Someone who didn't know my dad or what company I own. I want someone who wants me just for me."

Brianna propped her head on her hand and rested her elbow on the table, her sky-blue eyes slightly dull from the alcohol. "Wouldn't that be nice? Hey, if this works, we need to do the same thing for me."

"No way." Mari shook her head. "I don't want your dad coming down on my head for allowing his princess to mingle with the common folk."

Brianna gave Mari a very un-princess-like finger gesture. "Daddy's not that bad. Besides, it's not like I'm going to tell him."

"You tell your parents everything." Mari shot back. "You have a disgustingly good relationship with them."

Brianna rolled her eyes. "Oh please. Your dad thinks you walk on water. You have him wrapped around your little finger."

"Yes, yes. My dad's great." Mari made a little gesture with

her shoulders that was almost a shrug but not quite. "That doesn't mean I tell him everything I do. If I did... He'd send me back to boarding school. Or a nunnery. Do they even have nunni—nunniere—nunneries anymore? And who thought that name was a good idea?"

While Brianna giggled at Mari's tipsy slurring, Ellie huffed. "Well, *I* don't have to answer to anyone, and I'm ready to have a little fun. I've been living in a gilded cage for way too long. I'm ready to escape real life for a little while."

"Just be careful what you wish for." Whitney shook her head. "When you get it, you have to be able to hold on to it or let it go when it doesn't work."

Whitney spoke from experience. And Ellie appreciated the fact that Whitney and her men had had issues to deal with on their way to their happily-ever-after. Or happy for now. Or whatever.

"I'm not looking for forever." Ellie was damn sure about that one point. "I'm looking for sex. Hot, sweaty, *good* sex. And no strings. I have enough strings in my life. I certainly don't need any connected to men."

Bailey raised a half-full glass of wine in solidarity. "Here's to no strings."

"Don't count out *all* men," Whitney chimed in. "There are *still* some good ones out there."

"Good men are like unicorns." Ellie topped off her glass of wine. "They're only in your dreams."

"JACK'S NOT WRONG." Samson Perez shuffled the deck of cards in his hands. "I mean, I know it sucks, but assholes with money want to make sure the people who handle their money are as tight-ass as they are. And you definitely don't qualify as a tight-ass."

Rob took a long swallow of his whiskey to drown a string of obscenities. It wasn't Sam's fault that he was a constant voice of reason. Or that he was the first to show up tonight at the 859 Club in Old City.

A private club with a roster of members from Philadelphia's elite society, the building was mostly deserted on Wednesdays, which was why Rob and his friends had a standing date to play cards on Wednesdays. Their private room ensured they didn't have to make small talk with other members, most of whom were older and...well, boring as hell.

The only reason Rob had agreed to join this mausoleum was because Manny had wanted to. Another one of those rungs on the ladder Manny believed he needed to climb.

Rob set his empty glass on the table and tipped another couple of fingers into it from the bottle.

"Guess I should be happy about that." Rob sighed. "I don't know, man. I've been thinking it's time to move on. I'm not sure the money's worth the hassle anymore. And I can get the same rush from a cliff dive that I get closing a multimillion-dollar deal."

Sam shuffled the cards with the skill of a Vegas dealer. "So take a few years off. Travel. Jump off mountains. Someone'll always be looking for a smart guy who knows how to make money when you get back."

"Where the hell are you going now?" Chase Noble walked through the door, followed by Ryan Delahunt. "I didn't know you were planning another trip so soon. Didn't you just get back from somewhere?"

Rob tipped his chin in their direction. "Nice of you two to join us this week. Always good to win a bigger pot."

Rob's jab was good-natured and maybe tinged with a little

jealousy. Chase and Ryan had been absent more often than not the past six months, since they'd committed themselves to a relationship with the Snowden heiress, Whitney. Beautiful woman, though a little cool for his taste. Seemed perfect for them, though. And despite the unusual nature of the relationship, the three of them seemed to be handling it just fine. Better than fine, if their laid-back attitudes and satisfied grins meant anything.

Chase gave Rob the finger as he sat opposite him at the round table then accepted the drink.

"He got his hand slapped by Jack for being a reckless adrenaline junkie," Sam said. "Again."

"What'd he'd jump off of this time?" Ryan asked as he sat next to Sam, sliding his own glass across the table to Rob.

Sam laughed. "A mountain."

Rob shrugged. "It was there."

Ryan shook his head as Chase laughed. "I hope to hell you didn't say that to Jack."

Manny walked into the room at that moment.

"Of course he did." Manny's tone let everyone know how he felt about that. "I'm surprised Jack didn't have a stroke."

Rob shook his head, though Manny wasn't wrong. "Jesus, you all act like I'm an amateur. I don't have a fucking death wish. How the hell long have you known me?"

"Long enough to know what you'd say if I told you to be more careful."

Manny's level tone smacked at him, a reminder that Manny actually gave a shit about him. Manny was the brother he'd never had, his partner in crime since fourteen, when they'd shared a room at Fairhaven Academy, the elite boarding school every man in this room had attended.

Their backgrounds were diametrically opposed. Manny's childhood had been poverty and homelessness, his dad in jail and nonexistent, his mom drug-addicted and negligent. He'd basically raised himself until he'd been twelve, when child services had granted his aunt custody. She was the one who'd gotten him into Fairhaven on a scholarship. But it was Manny who'd had the drive to succeed.

Rob had only wanted to be back in L.A., partying with friends, drugs and alcohol as readily available as candy. His mom had fought those demons and won, and she'd seen Rob's future before he'd fallen down the rabbit hole. She'd enrolled him in Fairhaven and he'd been on a plane in two days.

Their first days as roommates had been a dumpster fire. Manny had considered Rob a stuck-up, entitled asshole with rich parents who spoiled him. Manny hadn't been wrong. And Rob had never met anyone who'd told him that to his face.

He'd liked that about Manny. He'd *liked* Manny. And after a couple of months, he'd won Manny over and, by the end of the first year, Rob had found his tribe, and they'd run the school until graduation.

Chase. Ryan. Sam. Phillip. Aric. Wright. Bastien. Grayden. Manny.

"Life isn't worth living without a little risk."

Rob must've said this a thousand times. It'd become his mantra.

Manny's brows arched. "I don't want to be the one to tell your parents and sister that the last risk you took was the one you're not coming back from."

Well, fuck.

"And on that depressing note," Ryan drawled, "somebody deal the damn cards. I feel lucky tonight."

Rob grinned at Ryan. "Married life must be good."

Ryan, Chase, and Whitney considered themselves married, even though Ryan's name wasn't on the marriage certificate. It was one hell of a leap of faith to share a woman like that, though Ryan and Chase made it seem easy. They were happy. It seemed like such a simple concept, but the change in both men had been nothing short of amazing. Rob would never admit it, but he envied them, probably for the wrong reasons.

Chase's grin made it clear Rob was right.

"At least Whitney's not setting up fake dating profiles so she can meet men and get laid without having to tell them who she is."

"Jesus. Who the hell's doing that?" Manny looked up from the cards he was dealing, having taken the deck from Sam. "That's dangerous as fuck for a woman."

Chase and Ryan exchanged a glance before Chase shrugged. "We've been sworn to secrecy."

"Not sure that counts, though." Ryan's grin widened. "I'm pretty sure Whitney doesn't remember she told us."

Chase picked up his cards. "She *was* pretty drunk at the time."

"Who was drunk?" Aric Christian walked through the door with Philip Girard.

"Whitney." Rob grinned at Phil, who swiped the whiskey bottle from beside Rob's elbow. "Who's apparently spilling secrets Chase and Ryan think we might be interested in."

"Guess it depends on whose secrets they are." Aric dropped into the open chair next to Rob and pushed a glass toward Phil, who obliged. "So whose secrets are they?"

Chase raised his brows at Ryan, who shrugged and looked at Manny. Manny frowned before his expression darkened with anger.

"No fucking way." Manny stopped shuffling, the cards forgotten. "*Ellie* did that?"

Manny scowled, brows drawn down as he looked at Rob. "Why the hell would she think that was a good idea? Jesus, Jack'll have an aneurysm when he finds out."

"You do know millions of people use dating sites, right?"

Phil's pale green eyes held wicked humor. "It's not like it's a crack house where she's gonna be drugged and raped. Ellie is a smart girl and, last I checked, over the age of consent—"

"She's twenty-six." Rob set his cards on the table, unsettled for no good reason. "Old enough to know better."

"Which means," Chase said, "she's more than old enough to decide how to live her life."

Chase's perfectly measured tone made Rob want to punch him, even though he didn't care what Ellie did with her life. Why the hell should he?

Yes, he worked for the company she owned, but he didn't work *for* her. At least, not technically. Ellie owned the company, but Jack ran Perrault Financial and had since Ellie's father's death. Ellie had been her daddy's princess, until he'd died when she was sixteen and she'd been left to the dubious care of her bitch of a stepmother, a woman Duke had married only a few months before his death. Luckily, Jack Octavian, her godfather, had been around to step into her father's shoes.

After Duke's death, Ellie had been a fixture at Perrault Financial. As a teenager, she'd volunteered at the Perrault Charitable Foundation. After college, she'd started working there. Two years ago, she'd taken over. She didn't seem to have much interest in the rest of the company, but she knew everyone by name, from the janitors to the board of directors.

Everyone loved her, and she loved everyone. Except Rob. She barely tolerated him, practically went out of her way to avoid him. And when she couldn't, she rarely had anything to say to him beyond "Hello."

When he was alone with her, Rob couldn't help himself. Needling Ellie was one of his favorite pastimes. It was just so fucking easy. She was all sunshine and light to everyone around her, especially Manny. But when she saw Rob, she froze him out like he was a commoner crashing her coronation.

Now you're just being a prick.

Ellie never acted like a spoiled brat. So maybe it just pissed him off that she treated him like a disease she had to fight off. He could charm the pants off a frigid virgin, but he couldn't get Ellie to smile. She and Manny had a much better relationship.

And maybe that's your problem.

"She's too fucking trusting." Manny picked up the cards again and started dealing, although Rob knew he was working on muscle memory. "She'll end up dating some asshole who knows who she is and, the next morning, she'll end up in a sex tape on Pornhub."

Trust Manny to come up with the doomsday scenario. Then again, the guy was a security expert. And she was too damn trusting. She'd get taken in by the first asshole who smiled at her and wind up paying hush money to keep her naked ass off the internet.

Fuck.

Out of the corner of his eye, Rob saw Chase wink at Aric, who made a sound between a cough and a laugh.

Rob turned on Aric. "What the fuck are you laughing about?"

Aric tried to look innocent. "Not a damn thing. Don't drag me into this. Not my circus. Not my monkeys."

"Not mine, either." Rob picked up his cards and pretended to look at them. "Why the hell don't you bust Manny's ass over this? He's the one who's lusted after her for years."

Manny gave him the finger, his expression set in hard lines. "It's not like that. She's a decent person. I don't want to see her hurt."

"It's not like she hasn't dated before." Ryan's tone held definite laughter.

"Yeah, that didn't turn out so well last time."

The edge on Manny's words was a reminder that he'd had to

deal with her previous asshole boyfriend. Trent had tried to make Ellie's life miserable when she'd broken up with him. Manny had shown him the error of his ways.

"Oh, for fuck's sake, just ask her out already."

Rob's back went stiff at Ryan's taunt, even though that's exactly what'd he'd thought yesterday when they'd seen her in the hall.

This is a really slippery slope.

"You know why he hasn't." Chase studied his hand. "We gonna play cards or not?"

Manny set the deck on the table and leveled his gaze at Chase. "Why don't you tell *me* why I haven't asked her out?"

Every man at the table looked at Manny. Except Rob. He watched Chase.

Chase met Manny's gaze head-on. "Because you think she wants Rob. And neither of you have the balls to play Rock Paper Scissors to see who gets dibs."

Manny didn't get angry often. But when he did, smart men cupped their balls and ran in the opposite direction. "She's not a fucking carnival prize."

Apparently, Chase was not a smart man. Or he had a death wish. Neither of which was true.

"No shit." Chase shrugged. "But according to Whitney, she's 'sick of waiting around for Prince Charming to sweep her off her feet.' Direct quote, by the way." Chase sliced a glance in Rob's direction. "Not that either of you fit the Prince Charming description."

Manny found his voice after a few seconds.

"Ellie isn't Whitney."

Rob's head swiveled to look at Manny, now studying his cards like they held the secrets of the universe. Did Manny want Ellie to be more like Whitney?

"No, she's not." Ryan didn't bother to hide his amusement.

"But Whitney said Ellie has asked a lot of questions about how our relationship works. Actually, all of her friends have."

"Guess that's to be expected." Aric threw a couple cards into the center of the table. "It's unusual."

"Yeah, but you'd be surprised how many other threesomes there are," Chase said. "I know of at least three in Philly. So you know there's gotta be more. It's not like people just come out and announce it. It's not really anyone else's business. It works for us. And if people don't like it, they can fuck off. I don't give a shit what they think."

Manny's jaw set. Rob knew Manny well enough to know what he was thinking. And what he was about to do. Manny had decided Ellie needed saving from herself.

"What name is she using," Manny said, "and what site?"

THREE

"Wow, you look…"

Brianna stared at Ellie, eyes wide as Ellie stared at her reflection in the standing mirror in her bedroom.

"I look ridiculous, don't I?"

Brianna's face screwed up into a scowl. "Of course, you don't. You just don't look like…you."

"Is that good or bad?"

"It's not good or bad." Brianna head cocked to the side, as if trying to see her in a different way. "You look…different."

Ellie scowled, her nose wrinkling. "Usually, different is bad. Jesus, I look like I'm fifteen."

Brianna rolled her eyes. "Let's not get carried away. You definitely look legal. You just don't look like you're trying so hard. Wait, that doesn't sound right, either."

Laughing, Ellie grabbed Brianna's hand and squeezed. "It's okay. I understand." And she did. She just wished Brianna wasn't right. "It's amazing what less makeup and different clothes can do. I feel like a completely different person."

"You *do* look amazing. You just don't look like Heiress Elise Perrault."

That's what she'd wanted, right? To be someone else for a night. If her reflection was any indication, she'd gotten exactly what she wanted. Dressed in tight dark jeans, a flowy blue top that matched her eyes, and a pair of black stiletto-heel boots, she felt different. It was a weird feeling, looking into the mirror and seeing herself in a totally different way. Anyone who knew her would know who she was. It wasn't like she'd had plastic surgery. But she looked...like someone else.

Would her date be disappointed? She really didn't look anything like the picture she'd used for her profile, but since that wasn't her anyway...

"Ellie? Are you okay?"

"Yeah, I just...never realized how I used makeup as part of my wardrobe. I put it on a certain way every day because that's how I thought I should look. I used to watch my mom every morning. It never occurred to me she was putting on a mask. I guess she felt she needed it."

Her mom had been one of the only females employed by Perrault Financials when she'd started. She'd succeeded in a firm dominated by men in a field dominated by men. Then she'd gotten pregnant and married the boss's son.

Her mom had always laughed when she'd told Ellie the story about how, after they found out she was pregnant, her mom had finally given in and accepted her dad's marriage proposal. It was only when Ellie had gotten older that she realized most people got married before they had a baby. Her parents had been happy and in love, but they'd been in their mid-forties when Ellie had been born.

"Your mom always looked like a model whenever I saw her." Brianna smiled. "Her hair and makeup were always perfect, and her nails were always painted. Now that I think about it, I don't think I ever saw her when she wasn't completely put together."

"Honestly, I don't think I ever did either. She wasn't a ponytail-and-jeans kind of person. Did you know my mom got pregnant before they were married?"

Brianna's eyes rounded. "No way. That just seems so..."

"Messy?"

"I was going to say out of character."

Ellie shrugged. "She used to tell me I was the best Christmas present she'd ever gotten because she found out she was pregnant on Christmas Eve."

"Aww, that's so sweet."

It was. It was almost like a fairy tale. Except for the fact that her mom hadn't wanted to marry the prince. A fact they'd bickered over for years before her mom's death. Helene Sweeney hadn't wanted to be known as the woman who'd trapped Duke Perrault into marriage. She'd been a proud woman, a self-made millionaire who'd thrived in a man's world.

"I sometimes wonder if my mom would be proud of me."

Ellie spent her days spending money she hadn't earned. Most people would kill to be in her position. Worth more than she could ever spend in two lifetimes. Able to do whatever the hell she wanted. If she could just figure out what that was.

Brianna wrapped her arm around Ellie's shoulder and squeezed. "Of course she would. Look at all you've accomplished. You're an amazing person."

But she hadn't really accomplished anything, had she? She hadn't built a multi-million-dollar company from the ground up. She hadn't worked her ass off to move up the corporate ladder.

"No, I'm not. I'm just a girl who inherited a boatload of money and now I dole it out like a benevolent fairy godmother without a wand."

Brianna smacked her on the shoulder. Hard. "You know it's not your fault you were born into money. It's what you do with it that counts. And Ellie, you're a good soul. Now, go out and get laid. You deserve it."

"YOU KNOW she's going to hate you for this, right?"

Rob's amused voice carried over the din of the crowd in the Old Town bar. Manny had never been here before. He was pretty sure he'd never be back. The noise beat against his eardrums like an icepick and a tiny man with a hammer was pounding nails into his temples.

This was much more Rob's scene. Loud music, loud voices trying to talk over the loud music, wall-to-wall people.

They'd staked out a spot at the far corner of the bar fifteen minutes before Ellie was supposed to arrive and they'd both been hit on within twenty seconds. Rob had handled the women and a couple of men, leaving Manny to focus on the door so they wouldn't miss her.

"She'll get over it when she realizes what a ridiculous idea this was. I can't believe she didn't think she'd be recognized."

"So far, I haven't seen one person I recognize, which is unusual." Rob sounded surprisingly serious. "This is a whole different crowd than we're used to. Younger. Different social status."

Manny's brows rose at that last part. "You're not usually a snob."

Rob shook his head. "That's not what I meant. I don't think anyone here has recognized me."

Yeah, that was unusual. In their circles, everyone knew Rob. More specifically, they knew who his father was. Here, he was just another guy, something Rob wasn't used to being.

"You could've stayed home." Manny swallowed half his double whiskey, eyes never straying from the door.

Rob's amused huff made it to Manny's ears just fine. "I figure you're going to need me here to pick up the pieces of your pride when she's finished with you."

Manny gave Rob a discreet middle finger without taking his focus from the door, which made Rob laugh again, louder this time and attracting the attention of a few women in their vicinity. Surprisingly, Rob either didn't notice or wasn't interested.

For all the ways in which their personalities differed, there were so many more ways in which they aligned perfectly. Ethics. Politics. Money.

And Ellie. Even if Rob wouldn't admit it.

"She'll get over it."

Out of the corner of his eye, he saw Rob shrug.

"She already hates me. This won't change her opinion. But she likes you. You sure you want to jeopardize that? I know how badly you want her."

A couple of years ago, after a few too many drinks, Manny had confessed to lusting after the untouchable Ellie. He'd been feeling no pain, and he'd told Rob all the dirty things he wanted to do to her. Rob had confessed to having the same thoughts, although his didn't include tying her spread-eagle to a bed and making her scream with pleasure. Since that night, neither of them had done a damn thing about it. It'd been an unspoken line neither of them had crossed.

So why are you really here?

Damn good question.

"It's for her own good."

Manny had a shit-ton of baggage from his childhood. Ellie didn't deserve to have that laid at her feet.

Rob laughed again, drawing even more attention this time because of a lull in the music. "I hope to hell you're smart enough not to say that to her face."

"I'm not an idiot."

"No, but you *are* in love with her."

Manny's denial was immediate and automatic. "Bullshit."

Rob snorted. "You're usually a better liar."

"I'm not lying. And I'm not talking about this anymore."

"So you don't want her to date, but you don't want to date her." Rob's chuckle grated against every one of Manny's exposed nerves. And there were a lot of them. "That's not exactly your best plan."

No, it wasn't. And Manny was a master planner. The fact that he didn't have one for this situation...well, that sucked. But he knew he couldn't let Ellie make a grave mistake, one she'd regret.

Manny's job was to protect Perrault Financial. Ellie was a Perrault.

And he'd protect her whether she wanted his damn help or not.

NO, no, no. This couldn't be happening.

"What the *hell* are you two doing here?"

Ellie stared at Rob Henry and Manny Bianchi, shock holding her in place.

She'd been so careful. She'd told exactly four people about this date. Her best friends, who she trusted implicitly and had been sworn to secrecy.

Whitney, Brianna, Marielle, and Bailey had helped her narrow down the list of guys who'd wanted to meet for drinks. It'd been pretty easy to cut at least half the men on the first pass. She'd been surprised how many had admitted to still living with their parents. That had been a deal breaker. There'd been even more with whom she'd had nothing in common. Still more had tried too hard.

When they'd finally cut the list to five guys, Ellie had made the final decision on her own, though her friends had approved of her choice. She'd contacted Andrew Schaeffer, dog lover and chef at his family restaurant, through the app and agreed to meet him at a popular bar in Old Town. At least, she thought it was popular. She'd never been here before.

She'd arrived early to check it out, grateful to discover it was every bit the young crowd Andrew had claimed in his texts. There were so many people in their twenties and thirties, she felt almost invisible in her jeans and flowy top.

She'd actually thought she might be able to pull this off without anyone but her friends finding out. And then *they'd* walked up to her table.

"Hello, Ellie. Nice to see you, too. Meeting someone?"

Rob's grin made her feel like a mouse staring down a lion. She'd seen that grin turn grown women into blushing, stammering teenagers. Luckily, she wasn't one of them. And if she was lying about that just a little... Well, no one needed to know.

"I am. And they should be here soon, so you two can run along." She made a shooing motion with her hands, wishing them away.

"Anyone we know?"

Manny's low voice felt like a caress, as if he'd run his hand down her cheek and just kept going until he came to her breast and—

Stop. Dammit, she couldn't let him distract her. Couldn't let *either* of them distract her.

"No, I don't think you do. Anyway, it was nice to see you, but..."

She squirmed in her chair, wanting to tell them to leave but not wanting to draw any attention. They already drew enough female attention, damn them. She definitely did *not* want them to be here when Andrew showed up.

For one thing, he might decide he didn't want to compete when he saw her talking to two other men. Andrew seemed like a nice guy. A normal guy. A guy who wouldn't know who she was, or what she was worth. A guy who didn't wear a suit to work. Especially not a bespoke Italian suit. Not like these men. Who both looked damn good in suits. And who probably looked even better out of them.

Grr.

"You seem anxious." Rob slid onto the chair opposite her, unbuttoning his suit jacket, like he was going to stay for a while. Then Manny took a step closer, boxing her in. "Everything okay?"

"Everything's fine." Or would be when they left. "I'm sure you have plans so you—"

"Actually, we're here for a drink." Rob leaned back in the chair, looking around for a waitress. "What can we get you?"

She wanted to scream in frustration. "Nothing. Because you're *not* staying. I'm sure you have better things to do than keep me company until my da—uh, friend arrives."

"Actually," Rob grinned, "we don't."

Frustration ate at her gut like battery acid as Manny grabbed an empty chair from the next table and pulled it up to hers. Apparently, they weren't going to take the hint and leave. She wanted to stomp her feet and order them to go, but that would create a scene, which she absolutely did not want to do. Not here and definitely not now.

Her stress level ratcheted up with every passing second. She wanted to wipe the smirk off Rob's too-handsome face with a bop on the nose. Then she'd really give Manny something to scowl about. Why were they even here? Were the stars aligned against her today? Was Mercury in retrograde?

Get a grip. Just tell them they have to leave.

Yes, that's exactly what she should do. But she had the feeling that would only make them dig in their heels.

Time to be assertive.

"Look, I really don't want to be rude, but you need to leave." Then she took a deep breath. "I'm meeting a date."

Why did neither man look surprised? In fact, Rob's grin looked more self-satisfied than normal. And Manny looked like he'd sucked on a lemon. Why would he have anything at all to be angry about?

Well, damn. They *knew* she had a date. She didn't know how, but they knew.

"Oh? Anyone we know?"

Rob's blatantly fake disinterest made her see red. Honestly, she swore she saw a tinge of red at the edges of her vision. And with every passing second, her anger became a hot lump that festered in her gut, threatening to pour out of her in a torrent.

"No." She had to force the words out from between her gritted teeth. "And it's time for you to go. Now."

Manny shook his head, his dark gaze pinned on hers. "That's not going to happen."

Frustrated tears threatened, but she refused to give these men the satisfaction of seeing her cry. So she ran through every option available to her. There was only one. She had to leave. She'd message Andrew and tell him something had come up and she couldn't meet him. They'd make another date. Or they wouldn't, and she'd start over.

Or maybe I'll just give up on this whole ridiculous idea.

"Fine." She put her hands on the table, ready to push away so she could stand. "Then I'll go—"

Manny put his hand over hers, and she froze. Or rather, she internally combusted. His hand felt huge against hers, the warmth of his skin seeping into her body like liquid fire. And the look in his eyes pinned her to her seat more effectively than his light grip on her hand.

"Don't go."

It took a moment for his words to register and another for

her brain to process the fact that she liked the feel of his skin against hers. She stared down at his hand, her heart pounding for some unknown reason. She couldn't remember Manny ever touching her before. Why did she like it so much?

With a sharply indrawn breath, she pulled her hand away, her gaze locked with his as she tried to hold on to her anger. It seemed to have scattered away like dandelion seeds in the wind.

"Why should I stay?"

Damn it, why did she sound like that, her voice all wispy and soft? Almost...sexy.

Manny didn't answer right away, his gaze steady on hers. Confusion swirled, her heart still skipping along, even faster if that was possible.

"So we can buy you a drink."

Her gaze held Manny's for so many long seconds, she felt like she'd fallen into a deep hole. And when Rob leaned closer, she turned to him, wondering why he stared at her with such an unusually serious expression. She rarely saw Rob without a grin or a smirk. Life was an adventure for him, one he enjoyed to the fullest. She secretly envied him. And the man was so handsome, her mouth went bone-dry. She'd always thought he was much more gorgeous than his famous father, with his thick brown hair tinted with shades of red and eyes so blue most people wrongly thought he wore contacts.

Her gaze swung back to Manny, whose dark eyes pinned her in place. He was just as handsome as Rob. Brown eyes so dark they looked black, southern Italian heritage written all over his face in the strong nose and full lips. Her fingers actually twitched with the urge to sink into his wavy black hair.

No. Just...no. This couldn't happen. Not with them. She didn't even like them.

Okay, maybe that was a little harsh.

Maybe that's a flat-out lie. Maybe you like them too much. And maybe you know you can't have them.

She'd always felt a tug of attraction toward Manny. And Rob was exceedingly easy on the eyes—

No. Just...no.

Shaking her head, she pulled her hand away from Manny's and pushed away from the table. Her only goal now was to get out of this bar before she made another horrible mistake. The first had been believing she could pull off this deception.

"I have to leave. I can't stay."

Not now. Even though she'd planned this night down to the color of the polish on her toes and the matching bra and panties she'd bought at the boutique at Haven Hotel. Which also matched the color on her toes. The boutique owner had looked her up and down then specifically picked out this set of lingerie for her. It'd fit perfectly and looked amazing against her pale skin.

"Ellie." Rob's low, raspy voice made her stomach curl into a ball. "We know why you're here."

She blinked, her breath hitched in her chest. "What did you say?"

Manny leaned onto the table. "We're here to make sure you don't make a huge mistake."

Her stomach curled into a tight little ball of dread.

"I don't know what you're talking about."

But she was very, very sure she knew exactly what they were talking about.

"Yes, you do." Rob's voice grated like nails on a chalkboard.

Heat began to bubble in her stomach. Fierce and confusing. It had to be anger. Not desire. Right?

"So you're here to ruin my night?"

"No." Manny shook his head slowly, deliberately. "Not at all. We're here to help you get exactly what you want."

FOUR

Ellie's expression made the heat in Manny's gut seep through his body. His toes curled, his scalp tingled, and his cock hardened until he swore he could hammer nails with it. That happened a lot around her, but it'd intensified over the past year. Maybe because she spent more time in the office. Or maybe because he'd spent years denying himself the one woman he wanted most in the world. The one woman he'd thought he couldn't have.

But now...

As she stared at him with undisguised heat in her eyes, he thought, *She could be ours.* He couldn't think of one damn reason why they couldn't make this work. The three of them.

His friends had been right. He'd lusted after her for years. And she looked like she was considering his proposition. One that had taken both himself and Rob by surprise, if the look Rob was shooting him was any indication. Rob hadn't known what Manny was going to say. The words had just fallen out of his mouth. Because they were the absolute truth.

He wanted her. He wanted to strip her naked and tie her to

a bed. Then he wanted to do all the dirty things he'd been dreaming about for years. And then he'd watch Rob take her.

Because he'd be damned if he watched her date another asshole who wasn't good enough for her.

Finally, she blinked, her gaze sliding away. But not before he'd seen her desire written all over her face. Her cheeks were washed with blush-pink, her sky-blue eyes wide, and her glossy pink lips parted. He wondered if she'd look the same when he went down on her. Because that *was* going to happen. He would make it happen because, holy hell, he hadn't realized how fucking much he'd been suppressing his desire for her.

For years, it'd been a low-grade ache in his gut, one he'd ignored. Except in his dreams, where he made her scream while he fucked her all night. Chase and Ryan's relationship with Whitney had given Manny's fantasies a dimension they'd never had before. He liked to watch, almost as much as he liked to participate. Usually that meant watching two women make love until he joined them. Lately, though, his dreams included watching Ellie come while Rob fucked her.

He and Rob had never shared a woman. Had never talked about it. Now, Manny couldn't stop thinking about it. Rob was the only man he'd consider sharing Ellie with. He trusted Rob, but it was still a shock to realize he trusted Rob enough to share Ellie and a bed.

As he stared, Ellie's cheeks turned an even darker shade of pink, and he had to wonder if she had some hint of his thoughts.

"What are you talking about?"

Her words came out haltingly, but she didn't sound scared. She sounded confused. And maybe a little excited. He wanted her to be excited. But before he could answer, Rob did.

"You don't need to look for a man to make you feel desired." Rob sounded steady. Sure. "We're willing to give you whatever you want."

Her lips parted for several seconds before she said, "I don't —I mean— I have no idea what the *hell* you're talking about." She shook her head. "How did you even know I'd be here?"

Rob's left shoulder lifted in a careless shrug. "Does it matter?"

"I..." Her gaze narrowed, then her mouth flattened into a straight line. "Yes, actually. It does. I want to know who ratted me out."

"No one ratted you out." Rob's voice slinked into her ears. "We're not here to ruin your night. We're here to make sure you get what you want."

For the first time, she looked unsettled, maybe a little worried. "I don't know what you mean. I'm here to meet a date."

"You're here," Manny leaned closer, watched her eyes widen even more than they already were, "to meet a stranger and have hot sex."

Just saying the words rekindled his anger. That anger wasn't focused at her. It was a part of himself he'd learned to live with, a part he'd learned to use to his advantage most of the time.

It fueled much of his drive to succeed, allowed him to push himself harder and further. It was something he and Rob had in common. They recognized it in each other. Other people might call it ambition or hunger, but Manny knew better. What he didn't know was why he was so angry. He'd learned to live with it. And channel it to his benefit. He'd learned how to turn handicaps into strengths. And one of those strengths, unfortunately for Ellie, was an unrelenting drive.

Ellie's mouth had dropped open at Manny's last statement, eyes wide. He didn't need to say anything else. He only needed to wait for her to speak. Which might take a while. She looked like she couldn't find the right words to express herself.

She would eventually. She wouldn't be able to resist the challenge he'd thrown down. Because while she might look sweet-natured and easygoing, Ellie had a steel backbone she'd inherited from her father.

Finally, she straightened and her eyes narrowed. "You have no idea what you're talking about."

"Nothing wrong with wanting to scratch an itch." Manny thought his voice sounded reasonable, considering their discussion. "But you don't have to look for a stranger to do it."

Ellie sucked in a deep breath as her eyes widened. In the next second, she blinked and put her hands on the table, as if to push her chair away. Manny and Rob reached out at the same time and put a hand over each of hers. They didn't hold her down, didn't exert any pressure. When she stopped, Rob pulled back right away, but Manny let his hand linger. When she caught his gaze, he saw just how much they'd turned her head around.

Good.

He'd made a choice. Might not be the right choice, but when he decided to do something, he followed through.

"We don't need an answer tonight." Manny let his fingers trail along hers before he released her. "Think about it. No need to make any rash decisions."

As if he'd shocked her, she pulled her hand away from the table with a jerk, fingers curling into her palms. She looked at them as if they'd grown two heads. Or offered to fulfill her sexual desires.

Wasn't that what she'd come here for tonight? To get laid? He'd just offered her a safe alternative to going home with a random man she'd picked off a dating website. Hell, he'd offered her two men. All she had to do was say yes.

"I already know my answer." She stood, nose turned up, as she looked down on them. Her haughty expression made Manny's cock throb. "And it's never in a million years."

Rob snorted and Manny's lips curled in a grin, the first of

the night. Her eyes narrowed as the perfect bow of her lips flattened. But before she could stomp off in a huff, which she looked ready to do, Manny stood.

She had to tilt her head back to look into his eyes. He had the almost overwhelming urge to lean forward and run his lips along the line of her neck. What would she do if he did? Would she run? Or would she melt?

He fucking wanted her to melt for him. He wanted to put his hands on her shoulders and hold her in place while he kissed his way from behind her ear to her shoulder. Then he wanted to take her clothes off and let his mouth continue down her body. His gaze followed the line of his thoughts, stopping at her breasts, wondering what she'd look like naked. He'd never really allowed himself to consider the possibility before.

It'd seemed disrespectful to her father and to Jack, who'd given him a job and paid him more money than he'd ever dreamed about as a street kid with a chip on his shoulder on a fast track to prison like his father.

But now...

He'd carved out a place at a rarified table. He'd fucking earned the right to want her. Now, he wasn't going to quit until he had her in his bed.

Slowly, he dragged his gaze back up to her face, noting how the color in her cheeks had deepened. Would that flush extend to her breasts? If he smacked her ass, would his hand leave the same color on those cheeks?

Goddamn, he wanted to know. Now that he'd committed to this, he wanted everything. Leaning closer so he wouldn't have to speak over the roar of the crowd, he put his lips right next to her ear.

"Don't lie to yourself. We'll be over to pick you up for dinner Sunday night. Seven o'clock. Wear a dress."

As her mouth dropped open in shock and outrage, he looked

at Rob and cocked his head toward the door. Rob's surprise quickly turned to amusement.

"I guess we'll see you Sunday." Rob bent his head for a quick second, grin in place. "Sweet dreams, Ellie."

Manny walked away before he did something foolish. Like kiss her parted lips. Or throw her over his shoulder and carry her away.

"AND THEN THEY just got up and left! Oh my god, I wanted to scream and throw things at their heads, but I didn't want to make a scene. I was so furious. I literally thought my head would explode."

Ellie topped off her glass of wine then passed the bottle to Brianna, who poured a sip into her own glass. Well, it looked like a sip compared to Ellie's glass. But dammit, she deserved it after the night she'd had.

Luckily, Brianna had been home and available to drink and commiserate. Otherwise, Ellie might've decided she needed to talk to Whitney and that could've been detrimental to their friendship.

"I still can't believe Whitney told her guys about your plan. I'm sure she didn't do it on purpose."

Ellie sighed. "I know. We were all a little... Okay, maybe more than a little drunk that night. And I'm not mad. I'm just..."

Just what? She wasn't angry or upset. She was just...

Excited?

No. *No-no-no-no.* Definitely not excited. Why would she be excited that Rob and Manny had ruined her plans, crashed her date, and then practically demanded she go out with them?

Demanded she allow them to give her sex.

Oh yes. Please.

"Disappointed?"

Brianna's tone held a question but, yeah, that's definitely what she should be. Disappointed. Not... Well, not whatever this was.

"Yes. Disappointed." She nodded, hoping she looked more decisive than she felt. "Exactly."

She must not have done a credible job because Brianna set down her glass and tilted her head to the side. White-blond hair slid like a sheet of silk off her shoulder, her expression a mix of disbelief and...pity?

Ugh.

"Hmm."

She should let it go. They were here to drink a little wine, relax, and watch *Bridgerton* for the tenth time. She didn't want to continue to talk about those damn men. Yes, she still wanted to throw things at them, but she didn't want to talk about them. Really. She didn't.

"Of course, I'm disappointed I didn't get to meet Andrew."

"But you're not disappointed that Manny and Rob showed up."

Was that a question? "Of course I am. They totally screwed up my plans."

"So you're *not* going to take them up on their offer?"

Why did Brianna sound like she doubted her?

"Of course not. It's ridiculous. They don't even like me. They just don't want me to embarrass the company."

"Did they say that?"

"No, of course not. They're too smart for that. They said they were there to give me what I wanted, which is ridiculous. I don't want them."

"Hmm."

"Oh for—What are you trying to say, Brianna? Just spit it out."

Brianna's eyebrows rose. "Are you sure? That you don't want them? Manny or Rob?"

No. "Of course I'm sure."

Brianna gave her a look that made Ellie want to drain her glass in one swallow and fill it to the top. Again.

"Forgive me for saying this, but you kinda look like maybe you do. Want them, I mean."

Ellie gaped at her friend. "It's a good thing you only have to walk down the hall to go home because you must be drunk."

Brianna's brows arched just before she picked up her glass. "Okay."

Ellie sighed. "No, it's not okay. Dammit, I don't want them."

Brianna shrugged. "I know. You just told me that."

"Really, I don't."

Shit. She couldn't even convince herself.

Sighing in defeat, she slumped into her chair. "Damn them. They've got me all screwed up in the head."

Brianna took a delicate sip of wine. "I don't think you're screwed up. I think you're in denial."

Her lips parted to deny Brianna's claim, but she couldn't do it. The words just wouldn't come. Did she want them?

"Men suck."

Brianna gave her a look. "Not all of them."

Ellie considered sticking out her tongue, but that would just prove she'd totally lost all respectability. "Okay, maybe not all. But they're not all Prince Charming either. We can't all be engaged to Randall."

Brianna rolled her eyes, her lips pulled in a grimace, a wholly foreign look for her. "Randall is far from Prince Charming. He's a nice guy, but he's not the love of my life. Our parents decided we were going to be married when we were children. We just haven't decided when we're going to tell them it's not happening."

"You know if you don't tell them soon, you're going to be doing it from the front of a church in a white dress."

Brianna blinked, eyes wide as she considered Ellie's words. Then she shook her head. "No, it won't come to that. Randall and I are on the same page. We'll tell them when it's time. And I know what you're doing. Stop deflecting. What are you going to do about Rob and Manny?"

"Well, I'm not going to date either one of them, that's for sure."

"Why?"

That simple question tripped a few switches in Ellie's brain. *Yeah, why can't I date them?*

"Because I don't want to."

Brianna's brows arched again. That woman could say more with her eyebrows than anyone Ellie knew.

"They are kinda hot," Brianna said.

There was no "kinda" about it. On their own, they were considered two of the most eligible men in Philadelphia. Hell, Rob was considered one of the hottest guys in the world. Together... They were enough to drive a woman to drink. Which is exactly what she was doing.

"I'm not going to date them."

"Then why don't you just go to bed with them?"

Her brain stuttered. And not because she hadn't thought of that herself. She had. She'd spent most of last night thinking about it. And dreaming about it.

She'd woken up cursing Whitney for making her relationship look appealing. Because in reality, Whitney's men were totally different than Manny and Rob. Who were not Ellie's men. But hearing Brianna so nonchalantly suggest she just go ahead and sleep with them...

Well, why the hell not? They'd practically offered themselves to her on a plate.

Because you'd be a pity fuck.

That little voice wasn't hers. It was her stepmother's. And even though she knew that was Rachelle talking, she couldn't help but think that wasn't wrong.

"Ellie?"

"Hmm?"

"Stop it right now."

Brianna's sharp tone snapped Ellie out of her head. "What?"

"You're thinking about Rachelle. You always get that look on your face when you think about her. She doesn't deserve to take up space in your head anymore."

Ellie gave Brianna a grateful smile. "You're right. Of course, you're right. I just don't understand why they would even care about who I sleep with."

"Maybe because they care about who you sleep with."

She shook her head confidently. "No way. At least, not Rob. He's a player and I don't want to be gossip column fodder. I don't want to deal with that. And I do *not* want to deal with him."

Brianna's expression said more than any words, forcing Ellie to continue.

"I mean, sure, he's gorgeous. But I'm not going there."

"Uh-huh. I notice you haven't mentioned Manny."

And there was a good reason for that.

"Manny's just...Manny. He thinks of me as another asset to protect. It'd be weird if we just decided we're going to have sex. I don't think of him like that."

Another one of those looks from Brianna, and Ellie threw her hands in the air, almost knocking over her wineglass.

"Okay, maybe I have thought about him like that. Once. Or twice." Or three or a hundred times. Same with Rob, but she wasn't offering that little tidbit up for discussion. Honestly, this whole discussion had gone sideways. "You're not helping. I thought you'd be on my side."

"I am." Brianna looked her in the eyes, her gaze warm. And just a little challenging. "I'm just saying, you're the one who wanted to meet someone and have sex. Two hot men want to take you to dinner. I get that you have history, but don't you think it's worth it to hear what they have to say?"

"SURPRISE! How's my baby brother? I'm so happy to see you."

Rob blinked at the women standing at his door at the ungodly hour of eight a.m. on a Saturday morning. It was just luck that he'd been awake enough to hear the bell ring. He'd only gotten to bed around four after a conference call with the Sydney headquarters.

Since there were only five people in the world who were on the security list to be allowed to show up at his door unannounced, he shouldn't have been surprised to see these two.

Blonde, beautiful, and showing the bump that would make him an uncle in three months, Sarafina Phillips beamed at him for a quick second before she stepped over the threshold and threw her arms around him, pulling him into a hug that he returned gently, his grin widening by the second.

"Safi, what are you doing here? Why didn't you give me a heads-up?"

"Because then it wouldn't've have been a surprise. Duh."

Throwing her head back and laughing, his sister walked into his apartment, leaving him to greet the other woman still standing outside his door.

"Hey, Nan. Come on in. Nice to see you."

Nan Mehta nodded, thin mouth curved in a wry grin as she

followed in Safi's wake. "I told her she should've called, but when does she ever listen to me?"

His sister's partner for more than a decade, Nan wrapped thin arms around his shoulders and returned his hug. It'd taken nearly five years after she and his sister had started dating to get her comfortable enough to return his affection. It'd started as just another challenge, but the love of his sister's life had become more than a challenge. She'd become family.

"I listen to you all the time," Safi said. "I just don't always do what you say."

"When do you ever do what anyone says?"

Rob and Nan said the words in exact unison, which led to a high five as Safi mock-glared at them.

"Hahaha. You two aren't as funny as you think you are."

"And you need to sit down." Nan pointed her toward the couch. "You heard the doctor. You need more rest."

"The doctor also said I need to get more exercise." Safi's hands went to her waist. "I don't think standing here for a few more minutes is going to throw me into early labor. Stop worrying."

Rob gave his sister a look before turning to Nan to ask the question. "Is there a problem?"

His sister sighed dramatically, but Rob was focused on Nan. His sister had had two miscarriages before this pregnancy and each one had left her devastated. He and Nan had been there to pick up the pieces, but feeling helpless was something Rob fucking hated.

Nan shook her head, and Rob felt a weight lift from his shoulders.

"No. She's fine. I'm just being me."

"And I love you." Safi sighed wrapped her arms around Nan and smacked a kiss on her cheek. "But you need to chill. Tell her to chill, Rob."

"I tell her to chill all the time, but she never listens to me. You still didn't tell me what you're doing here."

"Do I need a reason to visit my baby brother?"

Rob's gaze narrowed. "No. But you don't usually make cross-country trips out of the blue to do it." Then he noticed the number of bags sitting outside his door. "Damn, sis, you're not that big. What's with all the clothes?"

He almost missed the look his sister gave him as he and Nan brought the bags inside. And when he finally shut the door, he crossed his arms over his chest.

"All right, you two. What's going on?"

Safi and Nan exchanged a quick look as Nan put her arm around Safi's shoulders in support.

"Well, I've got an even bigger surprise for you." Safi smiled wide. Too wide. "We're about to be neighbors."

"ELISE, WE NEED TO SPEAK."

Just a few years ago, those four words would've instilled panic in Ellie. Today, she wouldn't exactly call it panic, but it certainly wasn't what she wanted to hear at precisely nine a.m. on a Friday morning. Or any morning.

She'd just sat down at her desk in the foundation offices when her phone began playing Darth Vader's theme music. She'd wanted to ignore it but knew the next time it rang, the conversation would be even more painful.

Might as well just get it over with now.

Easier said than done.

Her heart had stuttered, and her lungs had felt like she'd inhaled concrete. Evil stepmother strikes again. Sucking in air, she'd sat up straight and picked up her phone as gently as if it were dynamite. *Ugh.* She should be over this by now. Why did this woman still have the power to make her feel like an awkward, terrified child?

Because you give her that power.

She answered the call before she gave it any more thought.

Rachelle Perrault's voice stung like a wasp, even through the phone. "We need to discuss your sister Silla's allowance."

Rachelle never referred to her children as Ellie's stepsisters. But she never referred to herself as Ellie's mother, as if she realized that was a line she should never cross. Rachelle was barely a mother to her own daughters. Except, of course, when they needed money.

"Hello, Rachelle. You know I can't do anything about the amount of money Silla and Annie get from their trusts."

"Of course I know that." Her words cracked like a whip, landing with a sting. "I know very well how their trusts work."

Ellie flinched then mentally scolded herself. This woman no longer had any power over her in any way and she was no longer a grieving teenager.

"Then what can I help you with?"

"I would never ask for myself. You know that. But when it comes to my children, I'll do whatever needs to be done."

Ellie had heard this speech from Rachelle so many times, you'd think she'd be used to it. But no, she didn't think she'd ever get used to it. Her stepmother managed to intimidate, infuriate, and guilt her into providing her sisters with money for everything from shoes to trips to cars, all of which could be paid for from the more-than-generous trust her father had set up for the girls. Her dad had had his faults but making sure his family was taken care of hadn't been one of them.

When Duke Perrault had died in a car accident only three months after marrying Rachelle, she had gone from doting stepmother to wicked stepmonster in the blink of an eye. Ellie had to believe her dad hadn't known how much of a bitch his second wife was. Rachelle had snowed everyone. Even Ellie had believed the woman cared about her when she'd married Ellie's dad. Her true colors had only emerged after his death.

And here Rachelle was again, guilting Ellie into giving her money for her sisters, who had more than enough to live well. But Rachelle never let her forget that it wasn't as well as Ellie.

"I'm not sure if you remember, but Silla's graduation is right around the corner and her friends are planning their graduation parties and Silla's worried about where to hold hers. The girls at that school already treat my daughters like imposters…"

Rachelle droned on for another ten minutes, barely stopping to breathe. And every second that passed, Ellie found it harder to breathe. Why did she let this woman do this to her?

Because you're a pushover.

"…so I would appreciate if you could help your sister with this."

Ellie didn't hesitate. "Of course. Let me know how much and I'll have the money transferred."

The silence from the other end of the line was deafening. And just long enough that Ellie's temples began to pound.

"Well. I'm sure Silla will be grateful for your charity."

Ellie gritted her teeth against the urge to snap. She didn't do this out of charity. She did it because her stepsisters were in no way responsible for their mother's greed. The first time Rachelle had asked for money for one of the girls, Ellie had been only happy to give it, to be able to give it. Then Rachelle had continued to ask, and Ellie had continued to give. Her dad had left her with more than enough for two lifetimes. She'd realized early on that Rachelle would never have enough, no matter how much money was in her bank account.

"I'm happy to help."

Absolutely the truth. And yet so not what she wanted to say. But she knew that if she let Rachelle believe she'd won this round, everything would go back to level. Not normal. There was no normal. Rachelle would leave her alone for weeks, maybe months. She'd get the occasional text from Annie from college, just a few quick words to say hi. Ellie sometimes wondered if Rachelle made Annie text, as a way to keep in Ellie's good graces. Of course, Silla never did, so maybe there was hope for her relationship with Annie.

"You should stop for dinner. I'm sure the girls would love to see you."

Ellie contained a snort. Rachelle didn't want her to come for dinner and, no, the girls wouldn't love to see her. They were teenagers, Annie in her second year at college and Silla a senior in high school. Silla was the quintessential mean girl, egotistical and sarcastic, a perfect copy of her mother from her copper hair to her haughtier-than-thou attitude. Annie had changed since going away to college. Something had turned the previously chatty, airheaded girl into a quiet bookworm who rarely visited home.

Ellie had been meaning to take a weekend and visit Annie in Boston, but she hadn't had the time. She needed to make the time.

"I'll check my calendar and get back to you."

"Please do. I've got to run. Silla has an appointment. We'll speak again."

Before Ellie could say another word, Rachelle disconnected, and Ellie sucked in a deep breath. The knot in her chest eased and her muscles relaxed at once, until she felt like she needed to sit down, even though she was already sitting.

Why did she let Rachelle get to her like this? She needed to grow a spine and learn to tell the woman no. She really shouldn't care what the woman thought of her.

"You need to get a backbone, that's what you need."

And when she got that backbone, she would tell Manny and

Rob there was no way she was going out with them. Either of them. Even if the little devil on her shoulder told her to go, have a good time. She'd lusted after Manny for years, even though she'd worked overtime to make sure it didn't show. At least, she hoped it didn't.

As for Rob... With Rob, there was just too much baggage. She didn't even really like him.

Liar.

Okay, fine. Maybe she could admit, only to herself, that Rob turned her on. Maybe she should agree to have stress-relieving sex with Rob. Get it out of her system. But then she'd never be able to face him in the office, so she'd have to go into hiding. Which was ridiculous. If only...

"Oh, just don't even start."

Damn it. She'd said that out loud. She really needed to stop talking to herself where other people could possibly hear her. And she really needed to stop thinking about having sex with both of them, as if it were actually possible.

That doesn't mean you can't date one of them. They aren't attached at the hip.

Could she do it? Could she tell Manny she would go out with him? Could she tell Rob she didn't want to date him?

Would you be lying if you did?

She had her phone in her hand before she realized it.

"You have completely screwed up my life."

The husky laugh from the other end of the line was a familiar sound.

"And what," Whitney said, "have I done this time?"

"You know I love you, but damn it, Whit, I really hate you right now."

"Wanna tell me why? Or do you just want to complain for a few more minutes and then we'll pretend this never happened?"

"It's you and your men. You're making me think...things I shouldn't be."

"That sounds interesting. Who are you thinking these things about?"

"I can't believe you haven't heard already."

"Heard what?"

"Manny and Rob found out about my date and crashed it before it started."

The silence from the other end of the line was deafening for several long seconds.

"Damn. I am *so* sorry. It was me, wasn't it? I told Chase and Ryan, didn't I? Ugh, I didn't mean to. I don't even remember—"

"It's fine." Ellie sighed. "Honestly. I'm not mad." Not at Whitney. "I just don't know what to do now because I don't want to go out with them. Well, at least, not both of them."

Whitney paused for several long seconds. "I know you've had a crush on Manny forever. And I know you and Rob rub each other the wrong way. So tell them the truth."

"I don't want to hurt Rob's feelings."

Whitney's laughter sounded lighter than it had in years. Her unconventional relationship made her happier than she'd ever been. Ellie wanted a little of that happiness for herself.

"Don't take this the wrong way, but do you think you can hurt Rob's feelings? I mean, he is kind of a narcissist, isn't he?"

"No, he's not. He's—" *Why are you defending him?* "Oh, I guess you're right. I don't think he'll care if I say no to him."

"That's not what I meant."

"No, but it's true. You're right. I just need to say no."

Whitney gave a short nod. "Good for you. You say yes way too much."

"So you think I'm doing the right thing?"

"I think you should do what you want, not what you think

other people want you to do." Another pause from Whitney. "Do you want to go out with both of them?"

Ellie threw her hands in the air and rolling her eyes. "Honestly, I'm just not sure anymore. Everything's getting very confusing. Your relationship is turning the rest of us into idiots."

Whitney's smile was sly. "Or maybe it's just showing you there are more options than you may have considered before."

⸻

"SO THEY JUST SHOWED UP AND said they're moving here. Did something happen? Is your sister okay?"

"She's fine. Nan's fine. The baby's fine. Everything's fine. At least, that's what they said."

"You think there's something more going on?"

"Don't you? I mean, Safi said she was going to take time off after the baby was born and Nan can work from anywhere, but it seems out of the blue."

Rob shook his head then tipped more whiskey down his throat. He and Manny had stopped for a drink at Haven Hotel following a business dinner Saturday night. Their meeting with the owners of a smaller but prestigious firm who were considering Perrault for a joint venture had gone well. It'd been the kind of thing he excelled at. Talking to people, selling the deal.

But tonight, he hadn't been on his game. This thing with Safi ate at his concentration. He should be happy to have her close. He loved his sister more than anyone in the world. She was the only person, beside Manny, who had never tried to control him. She loved him unconditionally, without the grand expectations of his parents.

Rob glanced at Manny, sitting across from him at a dimly lit table as far from the bar as they could get. Manny leaned back in his chair, watching him. He hadn't said much since Rob had picked him up before dinner, which wasn't unusual. They knew each other too well for silences to be awkward.

Besides, Rob talked more than enough for both of them most of the time. Still, Rob knew Manny well enough to know when something was bothering him. And it wasn't Safi's reason for moving across the country only a few months before she was due to deliver her first child.

"What's eating at you?"

Manny took a second before he answered. "I've been thinking about your talk with Jack."

Rob shrugged, that conversation no longer of importance. He knew his worth to the company. If Jack decided he was a liability, there was nothing Rob could do to change Jack's mind. Manny trusted him. That's all Rob needed. If Manny lost faith in him...

"Nothing to talk about. He's not going to fire me. I make him too much money. Hell, I make everyone money. This'll blow over like it does all the time."

Manny made a noncommittal sound that made Rob look more closely at him.

"Are you seriously worried about me being fired?"

Manny's brows rose almost infinitesimally. "Of course I'm concerned. But I think I have a solution."

"I don't think there's a problem, so why do I need a solution?"

Manny sighed, a rare show of frustration. "One of these days, you're going to push it too far."

Rob shook his head, truly not getting what Manny wanted him to understand. "Push what?"

"Anything. Everything."

Swirling his whiskey around the glass, Rob studied Manny, who stared back like Rob was a bug under a microscope.

"I don't have a death wish, if that's what you're trying to say."

Manny lifted his glass and took a long pull on his beer before answering. "I'm not saying you're deliberately trying to hurt yourself. Don't put words in my mouth. I'm just saying you have an image problem, and I may have a solution."

An image problem. That was a new one. "Okay. I'm willing to play along, though I'm still not sure the situation is as dire as you think. What's my problem and how do I fix it?"

"Your problem is some of our clients think you're reckless. You need a stabilizing influence. You should date Ellie."

Rob's glass froze halfway to his mouth.

"What the hell are you talking about?"

"She'll act like a seal of approval."

"You've totally lost me. I don't understand—"

"Ellie is the most stable person I know." Manny leaned forward, elbows on the table, the seriousness in his voice intense. "Everyone adores her. She dates you, people look at you differently."

Rob opened his mouth then shut it. Because Manny wasn't wrong. Still, there was a huge problem. "She'll never agree to it. She hates me. You saw the way she looked at me the other night."

"She doesn't hate you."

"All right, hate may be too strong. But she knows exactly who I am, and she has absolutely no interest in dating me. And anyone who knows her *knows* she'd never date me. The only reason I went with you Thursday was for moral support. And to make sure you actually showed up. Dating Ellie has been your goal for years. I'm not going to cut you off just when you finally make it to the finish line."

"You know I can tell when you're lying, right?"

Rob caught back a grimace. "I'm not lying. Every word out of my mouth is the truth."

"A lie by omission is still a lie."

Rob shook his head. "Look, I'm not saying she isn't hot and that I haven't considered the possibility of a hookup. But she's your prize, not mine."

Manny's mouth flattened. "I never considered her a prize."

"And that's why you're the one who should be dating her. I'm literally going to be there Sunday night just to make sure you go through with it. We get to the hotel, you're on your own."

"I don't need you to fucking hold my hand."

"I'm not holding your fucking hand, but I will put my foot on your ass and shove you through the door if I have to."

Manny's mouth twitched a second before he started laughing, which was not the response Rob had expected.

Manny didn't date often, and not because he didn't like women. He did. Manny was just really, *really* picky. Rob didn't have that problem. He liked women but rarely dated the same one twice. Date someone more than once and she got ideas about longevity. Rob didn't do long-term.

Manny, on the other hand, was made for it. After the nightmare that'd been his childhood, Manny would make damn sure his wife and children would never worry about his commitment or their safety.

The problem was, Manny had met the right woman. He just wasn't willing to admit it. Rob was here to make sure Manny and Ellie got this right.

Manny's laugh wound down after another few seconds.

"You know, I'm not a fucking teenager who needs a wingman."

Rob grinned. "We all need a wingman sometimes. Hell, without me, you'd still be a virgin." Manny flipped him the bird.

"So don't think of me as your wingman. Think of me as your... fairy godfather."

The look Manny gave him was pure WTF.

"What the hell have you been smoking?"

Shaking his head, Rob got serious. "Not a damn thing. She's a good fit for you. I don't want you to fuck this up."

"There's nothing to fuck up. This isn't a goddamn fairy tale. She's not Goldilocks and I'm not a prince."

"I think Goldilocks had bears. And I think there were three of them."

"Well, there's only two of us." Manny fell silent for a second. "Have you considered it?"

Rob didn't have to ask what Manny meant. He knew Manny was talking about a three-way relationship.

"Not seriously. And only because of Ryan and Chase. You?"

Manny's direct gaze didn't flinch. "Yes."

Rob's brow furrowed. "Why?"

"Because it'd be easier."

Rob's huff of laughter was mocking. "How would a three-way relationship be easier?"

"We'd share the heavy emotional shit. You'd have someone at your back all the time. We work insane hours. We can be out of the country for weeks. Women hate that shit. If we share her, the emotional work would be split."

Well, shit. Rob had never looked at it that way. "I can't decide if you're brilliant, devious, or just crazy."

"So you see the merit?"

Rob shook his head. "Why would any woman agree to a relationship with two men who only give her half their attention and affection?"

"How would she know? If we do this right, she'll never notice a lack."

"You're not giving Ellie enough credit. She'll see through whatever story you tell her."

"I'm not planning to lie to her, and I'm not going to tell her a story. I want her. So do you. And you heard Chase. She's open to an unconventional relationship."

Yeah, he'd heard. He'd filed it away under "never gonna happen." But Manny had come up with a much different conclusion. And now that Manny had put it out there, Rob couldn't say he wasn't intrigued.

"How would you approach this?"

Manny's mouth quirked. "I'm going to lay it out for her."

"Are you going to ask her? Or tell her?"

Manny's brows arched for a brief second. "I'm not a tyrant."

"No, you're a bulldozer."

Manny didn't bother to deny it. "She'll either say yes or she won't. I'm betting she'll say yes."

"She doesn't strike me as a woman who's open to taking chances."

"And yet she was in a bar the other night waiting to meet a stranger for sex."

"A date isn't sex. I'm not sure she would've gone through with it."

"Your impression of Ellie is misguided." Manny shook his head. "She's not the sweet, virgin goddess you think."

"What makes you think that's how I see her?"

"Because of the way you treat her. You poke at her like she's a teenager. She hasn't been for years. No reason we shouldn't see her for what she is."

Okay, maybe he did think of her as a spoiled daddy's girl. She'd just turned thirteen the first time he'd met her. She hadn't spoken much, and at the time, he'd thought she was stuck up. But he'd been seventeen and an asshole. She'd been nervous, not conceited. And over the years, she'd grown into a woman known for being kind to everyone, with a smile that could light up a room and a personality to match.

It galled Rob that she rarely turned that smile on him.

"Why would she go for any relationship with me as part of it? You just said yourself, she doesn't like me."

Leaning forward, Manny his gaze intensifying. "I never said that. I've seen her stare at you when you're not looking. She's not sending you death glares."

Rob had his doubts about that, but there was a part of his brain that was buying into this crazy scheme. Telling him to go for it. What could it hurt? He had nothing to lose. And the reward could be having Ellie in his bed. There wasn't a damn thing about that he didn't like.

Manny, the bastard, started to grin when he didn't say anything.

"You really think she's going to want to say yes?"

"I think she's going to be too intrigued not to."

FIVE

"Are you really sure you want to wear *that*?"

Brianna swept her hand down and Ellie's gaze followed, looking at the dress she'd chosen for dinner with Manny and Rob. No, it wasn't the sexiest dress she owned, but then, she wasn't trying to convince Manny and Rob to sleep with her.

Would that be a bad thing?

Nope. Not going there.

Ellie glanced at Brianna, framed in the doorway to her room. Her friend's expression wasn't exactly complimentary as she looked Ellie up and down for what had to be the fiftieth time.

"Yes, I am. This isn't a date."

"Then why are you going? Just tell them you don't want to? It's not like they're forcing you to go."

Very true.

So why are you going?

"Because I know Manny. If I say no today, he'll ask again tomorrow. Or the next day. It's just better to get this over with."

"Uh-huh."

Making a face at Brianna in the mirror, Ellie took another look at her dress.

"You're right. I look like I'm trying too hard to keep them away. Okay, now what?"

With a sigh, Brianna walked to Ellie's closet and pulled out a dress without hesitation. She held it out to Ellie with a challenge in her eyes.

"If you're going, you might as well make an effort. Won't hurt to show them what they've been missing all these years."

"I don't know what you mean."

Brianna rolled her eyes. "Oh please. You know exactly what I mean."

Okay, maybe she did. And maybe that thought held some appeal. She wanted to stick out her tongue, but it was beneath her.

"You better hurry," Brianna said. "It's almost seven. You know Manny won't be late."

She looked at the dress Brianna had chosen and sighed.

"This is a bad idea."

"No, it really isn't." Exasperation tinged Brianna's voice. "Ellie, go out. Have fun. Try them on for size. If they don't fit, throw them back."

Ellie turned with wide eyes and a grin to stare at Brianna. "Who are you and what have you done with that sweet, innocent princess?"

"She's here to kick your ass and get you laid. And she's not that sweet or innocent."

Brianna grabbed the back zipper of Ellie's dress and pulled it down, making the plain gray dress bag and sag and look even more ugly than it had when she'd put it on.

"Or maybe you just want to greet them at the door in your undies and blow their minds. Wow. Is this from the Haven boutique?"

"Yes."

"I think we need to schedule a shopping trip this week. You'll probably need new lingerie for your next date."

"There's not going to be a next date."

FIFTEEN MINUTES LATER, Ellie admitted silently that the way Manny and Rob looked at her when she opened the door made her think maybe another date wouldn't be so bad.

Rob's perpetual grin broadened, and the intensity in Manny's gaze flipped from interest to heat in a split second. It was an immense confidence boost.

For a date that isn't a date.

"Come in. I just need to grab my purse and a wrap."

"You look beautiful, Ellie."

Manny's quiet words nearly made her trip as she turned to grab her things off the chair near the door. She'd never heard that tone of voice directed at her before. And certainly never from this man. She'd heard it from others who'd wanted something from her. Her money or her influence. Some had wanted her as a possession, as a prize they could win.

Manny's voice held pure, distilled honesty. He'd never thrown around random compliments, definitely never to her. He'd always been unfailingly polite, maybe a little distant. He'd never shown an interest in her, especially not a romantic interest. And now, he said four words, and she tingled from head to toe, her stomach fluttered, and her knees weakened.

Swallowing hard, she nodded. "Thank you. You look very nice." Her gaze flashed at Rob, who grinned at her in a way that made her think he saw much more than she wanted him to see.

"Hello, Rob."

"Hello, Ellie. It's nice to see you."

She didn't point out that they'd passed each other in the halls of the Perrault offices yesterday. Instead, she nodded and held his gaze, determined not to give him the satisfaction of shying away. And watched his smile widen...and become even more devastating.

Damn him.

He knew exactly what that smile did to women. And he knew she wasn't immune. She might not like him, but she couldn't deny the man was catnip. Pure, unadulterated, walking sex.

With an audible intake of breath, she took a step forward, forcing herself to hold his gaze. To show him she wouldn't back down. Because every smile, every word out of this man's mouth was a challenge. And she would *not* flutter her eyes at him and fall at his feet.

"I'm ready if you are."

She hoped those words were true.

"Is Bailey home tonight?"

Ellie closed the door to her apartment, then walked beside Manny to the elevator, Rob bringing up the rear. She wondered for a brief moment if he was checking out her ass but resisted the urge to look over her shoulder.

"No, she's out to dinner with her dad. It's his birthday."

"What are they blowing up this week?"

The smile in Rob's voice teased an answering smile from her. She sometimes forgot how charming he could be. "I don't think she'll ever live that down. It wasn't even a big explosion. There was no property damage."

"That woman likes to live on the edge." Manny pressed the button for the elevator. "She's lucky she didn't hurt herself."

The elevator arrived before she could respond and then the doors shut, enclosing her in a small space with two men who towered over her and around her, making her temperature rise.

She'd told herself she was going to play this cool. She'd spent most of the afternoon trying to get her heart rate to slow. Now, her pulse raced, and she couldn't seem to get enough air.

"I admire her." Ellie defended her friend. "She does what she wants and doesn't care what other people think. I wish I was more like her."

"Aren't you happy with who you are?"

Manny's question sounded innocuous enough, but to Ellie, it felt like a jab at a tender spot she hadn't known would hurt.

"I am." Mostly. "Aren't you?"

Rob huffed out a laugh, shaking his head, but Manny simply stared at her.

"If we were completely happy with ourselves, there'd be no room to grow. And who wants to be perfect?"

"Spoken like a true perfectionist."

Rob's comeback was almost inaudible, but she looked up to find him grinning at Manny. As her heart stumbled over itself, she looked away. Why did the man have to be so damn hand-some? He'd be easier to ignore if he was average looking. Then again, maybe not. Because Rob's appeal wasn't simply tied to his looks. His joy for living infected most everyone around him. Although lately, he'd seemed quieter. Less likely to smile. Except at her...

The doors opened, cutting off her view of Manny in the reflection, but she felt his hand at the small of her back. The thin silk of her dress allowed the heat of his skin to seep through, melting into her as intimate muscles contracted.

He didn't push, just let his hand barely brush her as she walked out of the elevator. It was more enticing than if he'd let his fingers brush against the exposed skin of her back. Her dress had a halter top and most of her back was bare. But he'd been careful not to touch her exposed skin. She couldn't decide if she was disappointed or charmed. She didn't want to be either.

When Rob opened the door to the black SUV only steps from the elevator and held out his hand for her, she took it without hesitation. And swallowed hard at his leashed strength.

Get a grip.

She settled into the front passenger seat while Rob climbed into the back and Manny slid behind the wheel.

"So where are we going?"

Manny started the engine, which purred like a big cat instead of roaring like she'd expected. Which was ridiculous, because Manny wasn't the kind of guy who had to proclaim his intense masculinity. All you had to do was look at him and it smacked you in the face. She wanted to rub up against him like a cat and beg to be petted.

"Friends of ours are opening a new restaurant. They're hosting a few friends before the official opening next week. Italian-Asian fusion. We've known the chef for years. He was two years behind us at Fairhaven."

"Sounds amazing."

"I'm sure it will be. He's brilliant and so is his wife. They've been planning this for years. We finally convinced them to let us invest."

"Where is it?"

"Fishtown."

So the drive wouldn't be long. Good. She was afraid if she spent much time alone with them, she'd be a mess by the time they got to the restaurant. She'd told herself she'd be fine. She could handle any social situation thrown at her. She could make conversation about absolutely nothing for hours and make it seem as if she enjoyed it.

But leave her alone with these two men and she was afraid she'd be tongue-tied. And wouldn't that be embarrassing as all hell. She didn't want them to think...what? That they made her hot and bothered? Because they did. But she certainly didn't want them to know that.

Then what do you want?

That was easy. She wanted what Whitney had. She wanted a lover, not just a one-night stand. She wanted an affair. A full-blown, steaming-hot love affair that made her so horny, she walked around the entire day with wet panties just thinking about what the night would hold.

Her idea to have a one-night affair had been ill-conceived. As much as she hated to admit, even to herself, that they were right...

"Ellie? Is everything okay?"

She blinked out of her thoughts, surprised to realize they'd stopped, even more surprised to realize they'd parked. Had she really zoned out for the past fifteen minutes?

"Yes, I'm fine. Are we here?"

She looked out the front window at the throngs of people walking along the street. They must have turned off Girard and onto a side street, because this street was little more than an alley. She didn't see any sign of a restaurant.

"Yes." Manny turned off the engine. "We'll have to walk a block. This is as close as we can park."

"I thought you said it hasn't opened yet."

Rob already had her door open and had reached in to help her down. "It hasn't. This is just Fishtown in the summer."

Taking Rob's hand, she let him help her out, only because she didn't want to embarrass herself and fall out of the SUV. And when he didn't release her hand immediately, she didn't pull away. Because she didn't want to make a scene.

Right.

"There's so many people."

Oh for heaven's sake. Could she sound any more ridiculous? She lived in this city. She knew how crowded the streets could get, especially in the summer, with the influx of tourists and the residents taking advantage of the nice weather. She must sound like she lived in an ivory tower.

"This part of the city's grown immensely the last several years."

Manny stepped up beside her. There wasn't enough room for the three of them to walk together on the sidewalk. The crowd was young and loud, laughing and filling the sidewalks.

It felt like a party. She smiled because this was the kind of party she wanted to be a part of. One where she wasn't on display. She might be a little overdressed in her silk designer dress, but not so much that she stuck out. Rob and Manny wore slacks and dress shirts. No ties, buttons undone, and sleeves rolled up. Rob's blue shirt matched his eyes and Manny's white stood out against his darker skin. Both had attracted the attention of several women and men, and she totally understood the smiles she was getting.

Lucky girl.

Yes, she was.

They didn't talk as they walked, the noise of the crowd too loud. Ellie tried not to look like a tourist, checking out the sights. But honestly, she'd never walked through this neighborhood before. How sad was that? She'd lived in this city all her life and had never really seen this part of it from this level.

But it was June in Philly and the humidity had begun to take its toll by the time Manny touched her elbow at the same time Rob put his hand on her waist.

Heat sizzled through her blood as she sucked in a breath. She couldn't see Rob, still standing behind her, but Manny's gaze narrowed, and heat drop-loaded into her gut and spread lower, between her legs.

Their connection only lasted seconds, because Rob moved to the door of the building beside them and held it open. Manny held her gaze for another long second before turning toward the door.

Get a grip. If you're not careful, you'll drool.

"I hope you're hungry," Manny said. "There's going to be a lot of food."

Oh, she was hungry. She just wasn't sure it was all for food.

SIX

"Oh, my god. This chocolate mousse is amazing, but I don't think I can eat another bite. You have to tell the waitress to stop bringing food. I swear I'm going to burst."

Manny lifted his coffee cup to his lips, mostly to hide his grin.

"You sure?" Rob leaned back in his chair, eyebrow raised in challenge. "I think there's something called Choco-Lavas Cake. Pretty sure Rick would want us to try it and compare it to the mousse."

As Ellie and Rob went back and forth on the merits of another round of dessert, Manny watched Ellie. He'd let Rob handle most of the conversational heavy lifting tonight, though he'd made sure not to sit silent.

Ellie had spent most of dinner raving about the food, which had made Rick, owner and head chef at Casa Bianca, her slave forever. Rick had been two years behind Rob and Manny at Fairhaven then had gone on to the Culinary Institute of America, where the man had proceeded to terrorize the chefs there for three years. When he'd decided to return to Philly to open his restaurant, Rick had had trouble finding backers until

Manny had accidentally run into Rick after he'd been turned down by another group of investors. They'd hadn't seen the potential in Rick's vision for Italian-Asian fusion.

Manny had told him they'd back him on the spot.

So far, nothing he'd seen tonight suggested he and Rob had made a bad investment. Not with the way Ellie was raving about the food. It'd been the main topic of conversation all through dinner. It'd also been the easiest way to keep the conversation going. She'd been quiet on the drive here and during their walk to the restaurant. He'd been worried dinner would be painful.

Then Rick had started sending out food. Amazing food, which had made the conversation easier. And Rick had been by several times to ask how they liked the food. Ellie had gushed, Rob had raved, and Manny had told Rick to hire more staff because he was going to need it. Reservations were already booked out for the next two months.

Rick said they'd have a table whenever they wanted. That could come in handy if they needed to bribe Ellie to come out with them again. Manny hadn't had a plan for tonight. Rob had told him to wing it, just see what happened and go with the flow.

Manny wasn't a go-with-the-flow kind of guy, which Rob knew. But Manny saw the benefit now, because they'd lulled Ellie into a false sense of security. And he was ready to close this deal.

She wanted an affair? They'd give her exactly what she wanted. Usually, that was Rob's expertise. Giving the client what they wanted. Ellie wasn't in this for the money. But she did want something. She wanted sex. That was easy enough to give, considering that's exactly what he wanted from her.

And if an affair with Ellie helped Rob out of the pit he seemed to be in, all the better.

"Don't you want any dessert, Manny?"

Ellie's question bumped him out of his thoughts, and as his gaze connected with hers, he didn't bother to hide exactly what he did want. And it wasn't food. Her eyes widened and she swallowed hard. Like she'd just realized how he felt about her.

Could she really be that naïve? No, maybe he'd just been that good at covering his feelings.

"No, thank you. I don't really eat sweets."

She was the sweetest thing here, but she wasn't on the menu. Yet.

A split second after that thought, her lips curved into a smile that made his heart pound. She couldn't possibly be thinking the same thing he was. And yet...her look gave him hope.

"But I could go for a drink."

He knew he'd surprised Rob by the look he shot Manny's way. The plan for tonight had been to loosen her up, get her used to them. They hadn't planned to seduce her tonight.

Maybe you need to throw out the agenda.

Just for tonight, maybe he should go with the flow and see where it took them.

"That sounds...nice." And she smiled.

It took them almost ten minutes to get out of the restaurant. They left a couple hundred dollars for the waitstaff, as the food had been free, then headed out. The street had only gotten more crowded. While they walked, Ellie held up her end of the conversation. They talked about dinner for most of the walk, but by the time they reached the car, Rob had started asking her about her classes at the arts center.

"I have a few students right now who are simply amazing. Much better than I ever was."

"Your degree's in music therapy, isn't it?"

"Yes. I knew I didn't have the voice to make a career out of singing or the talent to be a concert pianist, but I love music. And my students make everything worthwhile."

"You teach for free, don't you?"

She didn't answer Rob's question until they were settled into the car again.

"Of course." She shrugged. "There's no need for me to take a salary from the center, especially since it's funded by family money."

That "family money" was actually her money, though she never acknowledged that outright. Just one more thing about Ellie that made her unique. The woman's net worth landed her on the Forbes 500 list, but she never acted like a spoiled brat.

She should be a morose recluse with a chip on her shoulder. Instead, she had a sweet, sunny outlook on life that confounded him.

"The bar at Haven okay?"

She turned to smile at him. "Oh yes. I love it there."

His brows rose. "Do you go there a lot?"

"I wouldn't say a lot. I do a lot of shopping at the boutique there."

Manny thought about that for a second. "Kate's boutique?"

There was one of those smiles. "Yes! Do you know it?"

Yeah, he did. And now he couldn't think about anything but what she was wearing beneath that dress. She looked sleek and beautiful in a blue dress that clung to her slight curves but didn't flaunt them. It was sexy as hell. He'd managed not to ogle her all night, but he was fast losing the battle.

"Her lingerie is beautiful." Rob spoke when Manny didn't answer. "My sister will love her. I can't wait to introduce them."

"You've met Kate?"

"Yes. We've known her fiancé and his brother for years."

Her grin made Manny's back teeth grind. "I'm not surprised

you know Ty and Jed. Daddy was friends with their father. They were older so I didn't really hang out with them much."

Manny's hands tightened around the wheel and as he pulled out into to traffic to make the drive back into Center City to Rittenhouse Square. Exactly how well did she know the Golden brothers and their friends? Hopefully not well enough to have been invited into the Salon.

That's for us.

And when had he started thinking in terms of "us" instead of "me" when it came to Ellie?

Rob and Ellie kept up the conversation while he drove. Saturday night Philly traffic required concentration. Next time, they'd hire a driver. By the time they got to Haven, Ellie's laughter had worked its way into his head and all he could think about was getting her to laugh for him. Or sigh. Or whisper his name as he stripped her naked.

He'd been thinking about kissing her all day. How her lips would feel against his. How her body would feel pressed against his. The naked part would come later. He had a plan. He always had a plan.

By the time he pulled up to the hotel entrance, his jaw felt like he'd been clenching it for days. Rob and Ellie continued to chat as they made their way inside, talking about the architecture of the building. Manny followed behind, content to listen, checking out the building as they entered. Rob steered her through the lobby, toward the bar with its swanky, '50s-inspired vibe. The maître d had a table waiting for them, a fact that didn't escape Rob, who shot Manny an amused glance over his shoulder, careful Ellie didn't see him.

Yeah, he'd made plans. That's what he did. Sue him. Rob would be singing his praises if the night continued to go according to plan.

And Manny would make damn sure it did.

"YOU KNOW, I'm still mad at you two for crashing my date the other night. The guy never showed up and he never contacted me so I'm pretty sure you scared him off."

Ellie tried to be angry, or at least to sound angry. But honestly, she couldn't get there.

The past few hours had been the most fun she'd had on a date in years. Not that she'd been on many. When she'd dated Trent, it'd been more of a business arrangement. If either of them had an engagement and needed a partner, they were available. If they both happened to be in the mood that night, they'd have sex. It'd been good. At first. Okay, maybe good wasn't the word. Perfunctory? That sounded even worse. And their sex hadn't been bad, just...

Just what?

"We had your best interests at heart. We didn't want to see you hurt."

Rob's smile disappeared as he spoke, his expression dead serious. A state she hadn't been sure Rob ever reached. Even at work, in meetings or dealing with clients, he almost always had a smile on his face.

Manny had let Rob lead the conversation much of the night, which was their standard operating procedure. Manny hadn't been silent, he just hadn't been the one to steer the conversation. And while Rob never let a silence go too long, Manny seemed comfortable with it. He spoke when he had something to say. But mainly, he watched her. It didn't make her uncomfortable. She was used to being the center of attention and had learned how to ignore it, to not let it get to her. But she couldn't ignore Manny.

"I hope you realize I'm a grown woman who can take care of myself and make my own decisions."

"Of course you are." Rob sounded sincere. "We only wanted to make sure nothing happened to you."

"Happened how?"

Rob didn't have to think about his answer. "That you weren't taken advantage of."

"So you think I wouldn't know when someone was taking advantage of me?"

"I think," Manny said, "that you're looking for something you're not going to find from a random guy who doesn't know you."

Her body responded viscerally to his quiet statement and the tone of his voice. Her muscles contracted, the sudden, shocking reaction making her hyperaware of the man watching her so intently.

She turned her full attention on Manny. "And what is it you think I'm looking for?"

"Someone who makes you feel something other than luke-warm desire and scratches an itch. You need a man to make you drown in desire."

Her mouth dried as images flashed through her mind. Images starring Manny. He'd been a long-time fixture in her imagination. When she dreamed about hot sweaty sex that made her wake up achy and longing for someone else's hand on her body, she dreamed about him. But he'd never expressed an interest in her, and she'd never seen him look at her the way he was looking now.

Realizing she was staring, she blinked, her gaze flitting to Rob...who looked at her like he wanted to take a bite for himself.

Slow down. Take a breath. Can you really trust your perception now?

She glanced again at Manny, who continued to stare with the same look in his eyes. Swallowing hard, she drew in a deep breath then released it slowly.

Think carefully before you respond.

Because there had to be a catch. There was always a catch. Manny couldn't possibly be offering what it sounded like he was offering. And Rob... There was no way that look in his eyes was anything other than mild interest. He'd never given any indication that he wanted her. So what exactly were they offering?

Call their bluff.

Her chin tilted up. "And if I do? Want a man to make me drown in desire? What are you planning to do about it?"

Because she needed to know. She needed an answer to that last question so she could breathe again.

Manny's gaze now glittered with heat. "We can give you what you want."

She tried, she really did try not to react like he'd reached inside her chest and squeezed her lungs. Maybe she was hallucinating. Because she just couldn't believe Manny had just offered to make one of her long-standing fantasies come true. That he would actually want her.

Unless— Did he mean—

She glanced at Rob, realizing that maybe she hadn't quite grasped exactly what Manny was offering. Because there were two men at this table. And he'd said "we."

Could they seriously want *that*?

When had it become a sauna in here?

She wanted to lift her hand and fan her cheeks. Heat rose from her toes to her breasts, and she knew it must show on her face. Manny's gaze was locked on hers and suddenly she didn't care if Rob or anyone else was staring.

She swallowed hard and took a deep breath. And prepared to be disappointed. "What does that mean exactly?"

Manny's response was immediate. "It means Rob and I are willing to fulfill your every desire."

She felt her jaw loosen and barely managed to keep her

mouth closed when it wanted to drop open from shock. But shock wasn't the only emotion making her speechless. Another wave of heat hit her. This time, it flushed her from head to toe. It hit her so strongly, her mouth dried, and she wasn't sure she'd be able to unstick her tongue from the roof of her mouth to speak. But she couldn't just sit here and stare at them.

Deep breath. No more games.

Shoving aside her doubts and insecurities, she held Manny's gaze. "Are you offering to have sex with me?"

He didn't hesitate. "Yes. You want an affair. We'll give you an affair."

Oh my god. She turned to Rob, whose smile had completely disappeared.

"And you're willing to go along with this?"

Rob leaned forward, infringing on her space and taking up all the air. "I wouldn't be here if I wasn't willing to play along."

She swallowed hard. "I didn't realize we were playing a game."

Now Rob's smile returned, just a flash of perfect white teeth. "It's not a game. But I hope we can have some fun."

"Why?"

She wondered if they'd understand what she wanted to know without having to come out and say, "Why, after all these years, do you want to take me to bed?"

"Because we want you." Manny emphasized "we," just enough to make her realize he'd done it. "And you need us."

That put her back up. "I don't *need* a man to make my life complete."

Manny shook his head. "That's not what I'm saying. I'm saying you need someone to help you scratch an itch, an itch you can't trust to any other man. You can trust us."

Damn him. He was right. She did trust Manny and Rob in a way she'd never trust another man. She knew them. But she didn't know what they'd be like as lovers. Was she going to be brave and find out?

Yes, damn it. She was. Because she did trust them. And she couldn't deny that she wanted them. They were offering her exactly what she wanted when she'd gone to the bar the other night.

"How would this work?"

She wasn't sure but she thought she saw a slight smile on Manny's lips. And looking at Manny's lips made her want to kiss him.

"During the day, business as usual. At the office, nothing changes. We treat each other as we always do. After hours, we're lovers. No ties. Just sex. Whatever you want. However you want. All you need to do is ask."

She noticed he didn't mention emotion. Manny always said exactly what he meant. He was precise and deliberate. He'd have thought this out down to the last detail. It's exactly what she'd thought she wanted. An affair without ties. It's exactly what she'd expect from Manny.

What about Rob?

"And what do you get out of this?"

He exchanged a glance with Manny. "Manny thinks I need an image boost."

She shook her head, confusion making her frown. "I don't understand."

"He thinks I need someone to make me appear more stable."

"Jack read him the riot act the other morning," Manny said. "Some of the firm's older clients are concerned about Rob's extracurricular activities."

"You mean the ones where he jumps out of airplanes and kayaks down uncharted rivers? Gee, I can't imagine why they would be worried."

Rob's grin made her heart leap into her throat. "Does Jack give you lessons in sarcasm? Or does that come naturally?"

Her lips twitched. "I'm pretty sure it's hereditary."

Rob's grin widened. "I'm not going to stop being who I am. But Manny," he shot the other man a look, "thinks I'll be seen as more stable if we're dating."

She blinked. "You want to date me?"

Rob's gaze narrowed. "Why does that make you look like a deer in the headlights?"

She glanced away for a second, realizing he'd nailed her response. "I'm just..." *Just what?* "Surprised."

"By what?" Rob asked.

That you'd want to date me.

She wasn't going to say that out loud. Not even if someone held her feet to a flame. She'd sound gauche. And needy. And ridiculous.

"I mean, would anyone actually believe we're dating?"

Rob settled back in his chair, looking like he was getting ready to attack a problem. And the problem was her.

"Why wouldn't they?"

She couldn't answer that without giving away the fact that she didn't think Rob would want to date her. Except, of course, if he needed something. And, apparently, he did.

So she nodded and shrugged it off. And decided it was time for her to go on the offensive. "And would we be sleeping together too?"

Rob didn't answer right away, just stared at her with a look on his face she couldn't decipher. Could he actually—

"That would be up to you."

But did he want her? She had no doubt Manny did. It was written all over his face. She had no idea what Rob was thinking.

"And if I decide I only want to have an affair with one of you?"

Manny's jaw flexed. "One or both. The choice is yours."

Yes.

She wanted to say the word so badly, but it wouldn't form. The arrangement was exactly what she wanted. Why was she hesitating?

"What happens when it's over?"

Manny shrugged. "It's over. No tears. No ties."

Could she have them both? Did she want them both?

Can you give them up without having your heart broken when it's over?

A true relationship with either of these men would never work. Manny was married to his job. Rob would never settle for a woman who didn't have "Summit Everest" as part of her life goals. But for now, they could be hers. Both of them.

Could it be that easy? Nothing ever was. There were dangers around every misspoken word or wayward glance. Was there any doubt what her answer should be? It should be no. That was the smart thing to do. But with her heart pounding against her ribs and her lungs working overtime, she wasn't going to do the smart thing. She was going to live in the moment. Like her mom had told her to, just before she'd died.

"You're not guaranteed tomorrow, baby, so you have to make sure you live today."

She glanced at both of them before she locked her gaze with Manny's.

"Yes."

Manny's elusive grin was worth the knot in her stomach and the sense of impending doom that wanted to settle on her shoulders. And the shock that Rob quickly wiped from his face made her want to pump her fist in victory, even as she swallowed the lump in her throat.

"Then we start tonight."

Her heart stuttered. "What? Tonight?"

Manny shrugged. "Why wait?"

"I...I wasn't expecting this."

"Did you need to prepare?"

Manny's question had a humorous edge to it, but she heard the underlying challenge.

Could she do this?

"Can you perform on demand?"

Her question was meant to be a sarcastic dodge. But Manny cocked his head to the side, considering.

"I can look at you and be hard."

Her lips parted but no words emerged.

"Do you think I'm lying?" Manny's tone hadn't changed. "Would you like to find out how wrong you are? Give me your hand."

Manny laid his hand on the table, palm up. Waiting, his gaze locked on hers. Seconds passed as she considered her options.

Reaching for him, she expected him to slip his fingers through hers. Instead, he took her hand and slid it toward him. She had no idea what he was going to do as he pulled it off the table and into his lap. Shock held her still as he placed her hand directly over his erection, which she could plainly feel beneath the smooth cotton of his pants. He was hard, hot, and—though she didn't have a lot to compare him to—huge.

For a split second, she couldn't believe he'd do this in the middle of a crowded bar, but then she realized the long white cloth covering the square table hid their legs—and whatever else was going on—behind it.

"Does that answer your question?"

Another dare. Did he think she'd run screaming?

Holding his gaze, she molded her fingers to the bulge then

squeezed. Not to hurt. She'd never deliberately hurt him. But enough to show him she wasn't intimidated. Even though she was impressed. And wanted to strip him naked to see exactly what she'd be getting.

"I'm not easily frightened."

Manny gave her another one of those heart-stopping smiles that rivaled Rob's. "I certainly hope you're not frightened because I've got plans for you."

A slight movement from Rob caught her eye, and she turned her attention to him, her hand still cupped around Manny's cock.

"Do you have plans, too?"

"I always have plans." He shrugged, blue eyes full of amusement. "But I can be content to take a less-active role. At first."

At first.

"If you're interested in starting our arrangement tonight, I've reserved a room here."

Manny had planned for this. She wasn't surprised. But had he figured she'd be a sure thing?

Are you?

"Yes."

She didn't know if she was answering Manny's unspoken question or her own. There was no reason to wait. No awkward dates where they got to know each other. No fumbling kisses and tentative gropes because he wasn't sure how far he could go, and she wasn't sure she wanted him to. She knew exactly what she'd be getting.

Withdrawing her hand, which Manny had released, she glanced between the men. They exchanged a glance, another one of those looks that proved they could read each other's minds.

Rob stood and slid out of the booth so Manny could follow. Then Rob reached for her hand. She hesitated, until he grinned and leaned closer. "Don't worry. I'm not going to shove your hand down my pants. I'll at least wait until we're behind closed doors."

She couldn't think of a damn thing to say to that because Manny put a hand on her back. She took his cue and started walking, following him out of the bar and into the lobby, where they headed for the elevators.

She saw no one she knew as they headed through the lobby, not sure what she would've said to anyone if she'd been asked what she was doing here. It was pretty obvious she was getting into a hotel elevator with two men.

Her brain felt wiped clean, as if nothing could get stuck there. All she could think about was putting one foot in front of the other. Well, that wasn't all she was thinking about. She couldn't stop thinking about the feel of Manny's cock, hard and hot against her palm. She couldn't wait to get him naked and get her hands all over him.

While Rob watches.

That was something else she couldn't get out of her head. She'd never had someone watch her have sex before. Would she be self-conscious or would Rob fade into the background—

No, that was ridiculous. Rob would never fade into the background. He always stood out, front and center, in any room.

A shiver of excitement danced along her spine, her excitement edging out her uncertainty. And desire lit her blood on fire.

The elevator dinged the second Manny pushed the button and the ride to the sixth floor was silent except for the Frank Sinatra song playing from the speakers. Manny's hand remained on her back and the heat of his skin seeped through her dress and into her body, creating a chemical reaction that bubbled through her blood.

"Have you done this a lot?"

Her question took them all by surprise, but it had jumped into her brain, and she had to know. "Bring women here to have sex?"

Rob's cough sounded suspiciously like laughter that he was trying to cover, and in the mirrored walls of the elevator, she saw him lift his hand to cover his mouth. And a grin.

Manny, true to character, didn't crack a smile, but his brows arched as he met her gaze in the reflection.

"Occasionally, yes. Would you be more comfortable at my apartment?"

She thought about it for a second. "No."

"Have you stayed here before?"

"No. I've had no reason to."

"I think you'll enjoy the room. It's unique."

"How do you mean?"

The elevator glided to a stop and the doors opened without a sound. They stepped out into a deserted hallway with what seemed like very few doors. Manny directed her to the left as he pulled a black keycard from his pants pocket.

"This floor's rooms are themed. Each room is different."

Smiling, she glanced at Manny, who finally stopped at the last door in the hall. "That sounds fun. I can't wait to see."

Slipping the keycard through the reader, Manny pushed open the door and waved her through.

The lights must come on automatically because the room was lit beautifully when she walked inside.

And...oh. What a room. More of a suite, with a sitting area immediately in front of the door and the sleeping area at the back near the windows. There were no curtains, and the room overlooked the atrium that was the centerpiece of the hotel.

But first, she had to take in the room.

"It's like someone re-created a painting."

A sensual painting that brought to mind Victorian drawing

rooms. From the satin on the bed to the velvet-covered furniture to the paintings on the walls, all of which looked to be originals and not mass-produced knockoffs.

She wanted to run her fingers along the back of the couch and sink onto the plush-looking, four-poster bed piled high with pillows of all shapes and sizes. The furniture was dark wood, highly glossed, and the rugs were definitely silk.

"This is amazing."

"Glad you like it. Jed said his wife had a big hand in decorating this one."

"Annabelle? Well, that makes sense."

She glanced at Manny, who'd sunk into the couch facing the windows, then at Rob, who'd followed her farther into the room. She stopped by the bed, she and Rob now only separated by a few feet.

"Have you ever been invited to their private parties?"

She shook her head. "What private parties?"

"The ones they hold on the fourth floor."

Manny's voice held a strange tone, which made her turn and stare at him.

"I've never been on the fourth floor."

"Good."

Oh, now she definitely wanted to know what went on there.

"Why is that good?"

Manny didn't answer so she turned to Rob, whose grin held secrets.

"They're rumored to be...uninhibited."

Manny snorted. "That's putting it mildly."

"So you've been?"

Manny's expression gave away nothing. Rob didn't feel the same need to hide things from her. A fact she stored away for later.

"Twice. A couple of years ago. It's invite only. Kind of like Fight Club. First rule of Fight Club…"

"No one talks about Fight Club," she finished. "Is it really that secret?"

"You have to sign an NDA to get in." Rob nodded as her mouth fell open. "No joke. I'm probably violating laws just mentioning it."

She shook her head. "Is it illegal?"

"Nothing that goes on there is illegal." Rob shook his head. "It's completely consensual."

Hmm. "So they have sex parties?"

She really hoped she didn't sound like a virgin who'd just found out how babies were made.

Rob nodded, his gaze intently focused on her. "Pretty much. Yeah."

Sex parties. And both of these men had been to these parties. She felt like a complete noob who had no idea people might actually like to have sex in front of other people. Not like a twenty-six-year-old woman who'd had a few lovers and was about to take two more. Possibly at the same time.

Her heart began to race, and she had to suck in air.

"Sorry you asked?"

Manny's deep voice made her heart beat even faster. Not because he made her anxious, but because he made her horny. So very, very horny.

Shaking her head at Manny, she met his gaze head on. "No, just surprised you were there, too."

Rob coughed, and she glanced over her shoulder to see him fighting a grin, which made her smile. But she'd taken her eyes off Manny for a split second, and when she turned back, she found him standing directly in front of her. She tried not to be startled, but she couldn't help herself. She took a step back. And he took another step forward. A bigger step forward, which brought him even closer.

His gaze snagged hers, and when he wrapped one hand around her neck, she froze. She felt no fear. Not at all. She was ready. Waiting.

Wanting.

These men had promised to fulfill her every desire. She wanted them to deliver.

Staring into Manny's dark eyes, she tried to read his emotions, but the only hint she had was the faster pace of his breathing. This close, she heard the harshness of his indrawn breaths just before he bent and kissed her.

She didn't know what she'd expected, but it wasn't an almost gentle touch of his lips against hers. He kissed her like he thought she might break. And that was definitely not what she wanted.

She wasn't a damn porcelain doll, and she didn't want to be treated like one.

Lifting her hands, she ran them around Manny's neck and into the lush softness of his hair. It wasn't long, but it wasn't buzzcut and the strands slid against her skin like silk. Her fingers clenched, tugging him closer, pressing her lips harder against his. Trying to show him what she wanted and how.

But Manny wouldn't take the hint. He kissed her slow and soft. And sweet. He took her under by steps, moving his lips against hers, tasting her. His kisses drugged her, loosening her muscles until she felt disconnected from her body. The sense that she was drowning came over her in a wave until she had to pull away and take a deep breath. She blinked, trying to get her bearings, but Manny wouldn't let her.

He took her mouth again, and this time, his arms circled her shoulders and pulled her closer. And closer. Until her body was pressed against the length of his. Her head fell back to accommodate their height difference, but the rest of her body melted against his like butter on hot asphalt. And the erection she'd had her hand wrapped around in the bar had gotten harder. And hotter. And bigger.

Oh my god.

Her hips tilted forward, even before she realized she'd moved, and one of his hands ran down the length of her spine to press against the small of her back. He urged her forward, making sure she was completely plastered against him, no sliver of space between them.

She felt every hard muscle from his chest to his thighs, every bulge and slope. Her body reacted with a visceral surge, her heart pounding as he flicked his tongue across the seam of her lips. She parted for him, but he didn't immediately invade. He licked at her lips, teasing her, sliding the tip of his tongue into her mouth then retreating. Taunted her until she made a needy sound in her throat and slid her tongue out to meet his.

She'd never felt this wanton before, this frantic. As if she'd die, just die if she didn't get what she wanted. And she wanted him.

As if he'd read her mind, he slid the hand on her back down to her butt and pressed her even closer, until their clothes should've melted from the contact. Desire shivered through her veins like mercury, burning hot and cold at the same time.

Manny obviously felt her reaction because he pulled back, looking down at her, assessing the situation. She'd seen him give that look at the conference table many times, but he'd never leveled it at her. He was taking her measure, seeing if she was ready.

She was more than ready. And if he didn't give her what she wanted here and now... Well, there was another man waiting on the chair.

Holy crap. She couldn't believe this was her life. She was afraid she'd wake up and find herself alone in her bed.

"Don't stop now," she demanded. "You promised me whatever I want. I want you."

She sounded like the spoiled brat she swore she wasn't. That she'd worked so hard not to be. But Manny, damn him, wasn't giving her what she wanted. Manny didn't answer right away, but behind her, Rob laughed. He'd been so quiet for the past few minutes, she'd almost forgotten he was there. Almost.

Now she looked over her shoulder and found him lounging in that chair, out of reach across the room, a grin on his face but a look in his eyes that made a promise. That when Manny was finished, it was his turn. And he'd make it worth her while to wait.

That was, if Manny didn't completely wreck her first.

"What exactly do you want?" Manny asked, and her gaze snapped back to his. "I want to hear you say it."

Ridiculously, she blushed. She felt it burn her cheeks and stain her throat, mingling with the lust roiling through her body.

"I want to have sex with you."

"How?"

She blinked. "What do you mean?"

"I mean," he ran his hand up her back to her shoulder, then down her arm, until his thumb brushed against her breast, "what do you want me to do to you?"

She started to speak, then stopped because she didn't know what to say. She had ideas, so many ideas. She'd dreamed about having his hands on her body, about his mouth on her body.

"Come on, Ellie." His voice had dropped to a tantalizing growl. "What do you want?"

That was easy. "I want to feel desired."

"How?" He stroked a hand down her back and up again, a rough caress that made her want to climb his big body. "There's no need for inhibition here. Not now. Anything we do in this room stays in this room."

Could it really be that simple? Could she have him, have them, without consequence?

Be brave.

She could do this. She'd made a date with a stranger to have sex. Now she was being offered two men she'd fantasized about for most of her adult life.

"I want you to strip naked so I can touch you."

Manny's mouth curved in a smile she'd never seen before. Sweet and sexy and so hot, it stole her breath as desire whipped through her body, lighting her on fire, burning away the last tethers of inhibition.

"Okay. But ladies first."

She shook her head. "That wasn't part of the agreement. You first. Because it's what I want."

She'd get naked. Later. First, she wanted—no, she needed to maintain a sliver of control over the situation. Because she knew it would be fleeting. And that was okay. She wanted to give herself up to the fantasy. Tomorrow—and reality—would come soon enough.

Manny smiled again, and this time, it held an edge.

"Okay. Sure." He released her and held his hands out to the side. "Take them off."

He wanted her to strip him? Her mouth watered just thinking about it. But her hands faltered.

"Come on, Ellie." A challenge. "Be adventurous."

How did he see so much of what she tried to keep hidden? "Aren't I?"

"You've stepped up to the line. Now walk over it."

She wanted to.

So do it.

Taking a deep breath, she reached for his waist. Pinching

the fine cotton of his shirt between her fingers, she tugged the tails free of his pants, holding his gaze as she slid her fingers to the bottom button and working it through the hole.

A little voice inside her head kept telling her she shouldn't do this, that she wasn't brave enough do this. Well, screw that. She'd always been the good girl. Steady. Dependable. God, she sounded like a Labrador. Right now, she felt like a bad girl, and she liked it. She was not about to feel any guilt at all about that.

Manny had gone still as she took her time unbuttoning his shirt, each little disc slipping through the hole feeling like a major achievement. When she reached the top, she looked up to find him watching her intently. She fell into those dark eyes as her hands gripped his shirt just below the collar.

"Are you going to take it off?"

The rumble of his voice made a pit open deep in her body, a hunger that grew with every passing second. She was a little afraid that hunger would consume her until she wouldn't be able to control herself.

"In my own time."

Her voice sounded low, almost unrecognizable, tinged with heat and something she didn't quite understand. Longing, maybe. But that seemed like too simple a concept.

Don't think.

Good advice. She didn't need her brain engaged to enjoy tonight. In fact, it'd probably be better if it wasn't.

"You're thinking too hard." Manny's hands came to rest on her shoulders. "Stop."

"I was just thinking the same thing." She looked down. "I'm stopping now."

His shirt had parted enough to expose inches of tight, toned abs, lightly covered by dark hair. Her finger curled into his shirt before she released it and let her fingers brush against the softness of that hair. She loved the sensation of it against her skin, the texture. Silky but rough.

Running her hands up to his collarbone beneath his shirt, she nudged it off his shoulders until it exposed the upper half of his body. His hands had risen to rest on her hips, which meant the shirt wasn't going any farther without help. But his hands gripped her so tight, and she liked it so much, she didn't want him to let go. She almost felt like he was the only thing keeping her feet on the ground.

"Drop your hands."

It took him a few seconds, but finally, he let her go so she could pull the shirt down his arms, leaving him half-naked. He did a little twist of his hands to get it over his wrists, an unconsciously sexy move that made her internal temperature rise a few more degrees.

Did he know how hot he made her? Did he see the impact his naked chest had on her? If she wasn't careful, she might just lean forward and lick him. And that would be completely embarrassing. Wouldn't it?

"What are you thinking?"

Another demand. Another blush stained her cheeks. There was no way in hell she was going to tell him what she was thinking. Instead, she put her hands on his shoulders and soaked in the warmth of his body. He radiated heat, even in the air-conditioned room. It made her want to strip naked and snuggle against him. And she would. But first...

She stepped closer, her breasts almost, but not quite, touching his abs. Petting her hands down his chest, she leaned forward until she could brush the tip of her nose against the soft skin of his neck and breathe in. God, he smelled amazing. She wanted to bite him.

In the next second, she opened her mouth and flicked her

tongue along his collarbone. And smiled when she heard him groan deep in his chest.

"Ellie."

His tone held a warning, which she chose to ignore. He'd told her she had the control. She was going to take him at his word.

Gaining confidence by the second, she stroked her hands down his abs, hard and ridged. Her fingers played along the defined muscles as she trailed her mouth along his skin, her tongue dipping into the hollow at his throat before continuing on her way. Again, she ran her tongue along his skin but this time, she ran it up to his left ear, then took the lobe between her teeth and bit down. Not hard. Just enough to feel it give.

His hands clamped around her hips, as if he were going to stop her. Before he could, she asked, "Did you mean what you said? That I only have to ask for what I want?"

He paused. "Of course."

She gathered her courage. "Then I want you to treat me like a woman you want."

He paused, his body going still.

"Do you think I don't want you?"

He sounded guarded, cautious. So unlike himself.

She looked up, found his narrowed gaze laser-focused on her. Swallowing hard, she tried not to lose her nerve. How did he manage to do this to her?

"Honestly? I can't tell."

Behind her, she heard Rob snort, reminding her again that they weren't the only ones in the room. Manny ignored him.

"Are you really sure you want to know?"

She nodded, needing to hear his answer more than anything. "I wouldn't have asked if I didn't."

His gaze narrowed even more, his hands fastening onto her hips, tighter, until she wouldn't be able to get away unless he allowed it. She hadn't known how much she'd like that until he'd done it.

"Yes. I want you. Is that what you wanted to hear?"

Honestly, she hadn't known what she'd wanted him to say. She been prepared for him to say no. To tap dance his way around an answer. Or worse, let her down easy.

"I don't…" She stopped, wanted to make sure she said this right. "Yes. It is. I've wanted you for years. I thought you didn't want anything to do with me. Why didn't you ask me out before now?"

"Do you really want to have this conversation now? Or can it wait until after we exhaust ourselves in bed? I want it to be the latter, but you're calling the shots tonight."

Was she? Suddenly, it didn't feel like she was in control.

"You're right. It can wait."

Her hands had been resting on his shoulders—she had no idea when she'd moved them there—but now she let them trail down his chest. She took her own sweet time, her fingertips grazing his nipples, tight and hard beneath the dark hair. She heard him suck in a hard breath, felt his chest rise and fall against her hands. Knowing he wanted her, had wanted her, gave a whole different perspective on what she wanted.

She wanted to break him down, just a little. Make him lose some of that rigid control that ruled his life.

He always seemed so in control. What would he be like without it? She wanted to know. Wanted to be the one to make him lose it. She wasn't sure she could, but damn it, she was going to try.

Their gazes still connected, she let her fingers fall farther, over his abs, chiseled and hard, to the waistband of his pants. She wanted to flick the button open and see what he wore underneath. She didn't think he went commando, but was it boxers or briefs?

"You're so beautiful."

The words slipped out before she'd realized she was thinking them, and his lips quirked into a lopsided grin.

"Not exactly how I'd describe myself."

"Your body is like a work of art." She ran her fingers along the ridges of his abs. "Beautiful."

She let her gaze fall to follow the path of her fingers. Everywhere she touched him he was hard, his skin silky and hot. And with every passing second, it got harder and harder to breathe.

Out of the corner of her eye, she saw Rob shift in his chair. An electric thrill ran up her spine. She wanted to drive Rob crazy, as well. Wanted to tease. Wanted him to want her too. She considered for a second that she was going to regret this tomorrow. That in the light of day it would seem cheap. And she'd feel ridiculous.

Then Manny put his hands on her ass and jerked her hips forward, his erection once again pressing against her belly.

"Stop thinking so hard. Kiss me again."

She tilted her head back, not sure what to say to that, but found her mouth covered by his. The second he kissed her, she shut off her brain and gave him permission. For anything he wanted.

MANNY FELT the second Ellie gave over control.

He wasn't sure she'd meant to do it. Didn't know if she even realized. But now that she had, he wasn't giving it back. She wanted to be taken. He couldn't fucking wait.

He prized her lips open wider and invaded her mouth with his tongue. He took what he'd been dreaming about for years. He kissed her and kissed her and kept kissing her, his lips moving against hers, his tongue sliding along hers, teasing, taunting. She responded by allowing him to kiss her deeper and harder.

Damn, she was sweet. And hot. And he wanted to strip her naked, lay her out on the couch...and have Rob hold her down while he took her.

Lust rushed through his body, electrifying every nerve ending and making his cock throb. The image in his head lingered, knowing Rob was watching now. Rob hadn't said a word or made a sound, but Manny felt the weight of his gaze, watching them. It added a hint of the forbidden to what they were doing.

Did she feel it too? Did it make her want to push even more limits?

His hands, which had been spread across her ass, slid up to her waist. His fingers found the tie at her waist that held her dress together and tugged on the bow. He tilted his head, getting a better angle on her mouth, distracting her from the fact that her dress was splitting open.

But because he was kissing her, he couldn't see her. And he wanted to see her.

Releasing her mouth, he pulled back, just enough to be able to look down. He noticed how her eyes were slow to open, how her lips remained parted, puffy, and slick.

He'd kiss her again, but first... He lifted his hands and pushed the dress away from her shoulders, exposing her body. God damn, she looked like candy. And he wanted to gorge himself on her sweetness.

Her bra was pink, a pale blush lace so fine it made him want to lick it and see if it melted on his tongue like spun sugar. Her breasts quivered with each breath, begging him to touch her.

Her bra disappeared beneath his hands, the silk smooth against his palms. Her breasts weren't big, but they were firm. Her nipples poked against his skin, and when he squeezed her, she drew in a deep breath, pushing the mounds more firmly into his hands.

The little sound she made in her throat affected him like a punch to the gut. It was needy and sweet and, holy fuck, so hot.

He was going to devour her.

His lips fell on hers again, more demanding now. His thumbs brushed against her nipples. She moaned into his mouth each time he flicked the hard little nubs, her hands clutching at his shoulders. Her nails dug into his skin, not hard enough to hurt but enough to make him want more.

He pulled away. "Drop your hands."

She blinked up at him, startled by the roughness of his voice, but she followed his command. And it had been a command. As her hands fell to her side, the dress slid into a pile on the floor at her feet.

Rob's quiet "Fuck" echoed through the room, and she turned her head to look at him, but Manny caught her chin in his fingers.

"No. I want your attention here. With me."

Rob would have her later. Right now, she was his.

Her eyes widened at the rough edge of his voice, and she stilled, almost like a deer in the headlights. He wondered if he'd pushed her too far, but then she sucked her bottom lip between her lips and nodded.

Jesus, he needed to watch the dominance or he'd be ordering her onto her knees to suck him.

And that would be bad...why?

He didn't have a clue at the moment, because his brain had short-circuited. He was going on instinct now. And instinct demanded he grab her around the waist and lift her against him. Which he did.

Ellie wrapped her legs around his waist and her arms around his shoulders and tilted her head for his kiss.

His need for her was punishing, a building pressure. Lowering his mouth to hers, he released a little of that pressure by kissing her, sucking at her lips and grabbing her ass to hold her against him. He barely noticed her weight, just the rounded fullness of her ass in his hands and the glide of her tongue against his. She gave him everything he wanted. Eagerly. Easily.

Lust detonated like a bomb in his gut, burning through his body. Using one arm wrapped around her waist to hold her, he dragged the other up her back. He pinched the clasp on her bra open then ran his hand into her hair. The long strands slid through his fingers like silk, a potent aphrodisiac.

He cupped the back of her head, tilting her to get a better angle on her mouth, to get deeper. He wanted to own all of her, to be so deep inside her she'd feel him for days. So she wouldn't forget him.

She gave him what he wanted. Gave him her mouth and her trust. And her body.

Turning, he broke the kiss to walk to the bed, her heavy breaths caressing his skin, raising gooseflesh and making his own lungs struggle for air.

Ripping down the bed covers, he laid her out on the wine-red silk sheets. Her hair fanned out around her head and shoulders, her skin looking even more pale against the dark sheets. She stared up at him, no nerves visible. Only desire.

Good. Because he was going to push her even farther.

Holding her gaze, he leaned over and plucked the bra straps off her shoulders, tugging them down. She lifted her arms, reaching toward him. The motion made her look like she was beckoning him forward. His first instinct was to fall on her, seal his mouth over hers and take her hard and fast. The urge was strong, but he clenched his hands into fists and held his ground. He had so much more he wanted to do before he sank inside her. Because he knew when he got inside her, it'd be over way too fucking soon.

He'd wanted her for too long to be satisfied with just a couple of minutes. He wanted to go the whole fucking night. And that meant he'd need help.

Dropping her bra on the floor beside him, he reached for the matching panties that threatened to derail the whole damn plan. They were practically see-through. But not completely. They revealed just enough to make a man die a little inside. And he certainly felt like he was fucking dying.

She lifted her hips just enough that he could pull them down her legs, baring her mound and the fine, dark blond hair covering it. He wanted to rub the tip of his nose against her there, breathe her in. However, her clenched thighs blocked his view of her pussy. Modesty or tease? He didn't care. Just another hurdle to climb. Sign him up for the fucking Olympics.

Stepping up to the side of the bed, he unbuckled his belt, undid the button and released the zipper, the sound of the metal teeth releasing drawing her gaze down his body. His abs clenched hard when she stared at his crotch. Her teeth lodged in her bottom lip as she rose onto her elbows. Waiting for him to continue.

He'd never stripped for a woman. Had never cared to. But the way Ellie was staring at him...

Fuck it.

He shoved his pants and boxers down his thighs and to his feet, toeing off his shoes before he bent to strip off his socks. Stepping out of his pants, he crawled onto the bed, his knees on either side of her hips. He grinned at the desire on her face as she stared at his erection then let her gaze take its own sweet time to travel up his body until she stared into his eyes again.

The tiny, wicked grin on her lips was a siren's call. Bending over her, he cupped her head in his hands and lifted her to meet his lips. She kissed him with so much passion, so much want, he nearly gave in and took what she was offering.

No.

Pulling away, he said one word.

"Rob."

Her eyes widened, startled but not afraid. Eager.

Rob didn't answer, but Ellie's eyes darted to the side. Manny watched for rejection or, worse, fear. He didn't see any hint of hesitation, only that bright-eyed excitement.

"Grab her hands."

Manny didn't have to say anything else. Rob knew what he wanted.

On the other side of the bed now, Rob sat on the edge and reached for her hands, currently resting on Manny's shoulders. He pulled them over her head slowly then held them with one hand on his thigh. When her hands made contact, she sucked in a short, sharp breath, making her breasts shimmy. And Manny's blood pressure skyrocket.

"If you don't want to do something, I expect you to say so. Otherwise, we're—"

"I'll tell you if I don't like what you're doing." Her voice was breathless, but her gaze met his directly. "Don't stop."

The one last restraint he'd been holding snapped, his brain shutting down the niggling voice that kept saying this was a bad idea. Because it wasn't. Nothing that felt this fucking good could be bad.

Planting his fists on either side of her head, he leaned down and sealed their mouths together again. This time, she lifted to meet his lips, her head tilting slightly to get the angle perfect. When his mouth opened over hers, her tongue slid past his lips to tangle and dance with his. And her hips arched to rub her pussy against his cock. She didn't quite reach, but he felt the motion of her body and her intent. It'd be so easy to spread her legs and sink inside her. But he wanted more than to fuck her. He wanted to make her come so many different ways, she wouldn't be sure which way was up when they were done.

While they kissed, he lifted his right hand from the bed to cup one perfect breast. She fit into his palm like she'd been made for him. Plumping her soft flesh, he squeezed, felt her give a little gasp into his mouth, felt her body stiffen, as if she were trying to get Rob to release her. Wasn't going to happen. Rob wouldn't hurt her, but he wasn't going to let her go.

He pulled back, shooting a glance at Rob, whose attention was fully focused on Ellie. So Manny would give him something to watch.

He tweaked her nipple, not hard enough to hurt, but by no means gentle. Her moan let him know he was on the right track. Switching to her other breast, he gave that the same treatment.

God damn, she was soft, so fucking soft, and she kissed him like he'd dreamed about her doing for years. Like she wanted to devour him.

Me first.

He sank deeper into the kiss, playing with her breasts until he felt her straining against Rob's hold and pushing herself farther into his hands. His control slipped out of his grasp, and he sank down onto her body, spreading himself out on top of her.

The feel of her naked body against his made him groan with pleasure. His aching cock pressed against her stomach, and it took everything he had not to grind his erection against her silky skin until he came. But he didn't want to shoot his load all over her stomach. He wanted to fill her with it.

Which couldn't happen. He couldn't take her without a condom. He wanted to. Fuck, did he want to. But that wasn't happening. At least, not this time.

Next time. There'd definitely be a next time.

But for now...

He heard the faint scrape of wood on wood as he wedged his knees between hers and spread her legs. He had so much more to explore before he got inside her but, damn, he couldn't stop. It felt like a compulsion, all-consuming. He'd never felt this way about a woman. Like he wanted to brand her as his.

It was a foreign concept, to want to claim a woman. Especially because he knew he'd be sharing her.

Fuck.

He broke the kiss, her protesting moan and the way her body twisted nearly making him falter. But he wanted to taste her, all of her.

His mouth slid down her throat, stopping to suck on the junction between her neck and shoulder. She shuddered, the sound she made throwing more fuel on his fast-burning desire. While he held himself above her with one hand, the other skimmed down her body to her hips, pinning her in place. She tried to twist beneath him, her body trying to rise up to meet his. But he knew if she did, his resolve would be toast. He'd fuck her hard and fast. He didn't want that for their first time.

His mouth continued lower, to her breasts. He sucked on her nipples, alternating between the two while she tried to arch her back, offering more of herself to him. Coming up onto his knees freed both of his hands, and he cupped her breasts, squeezing the small mounds until she said, "Please."

He didn't need to hear more to know what she wanted. He opened his mouth and drew one nipple between his teeth, letting them sink into the soft flesh. She responded by arching her back, giving him more. Alternating between breasts, he teased her mercilessly, giving her no time to take a breath, to allow her desire to falter in any way.

He couldn't seem to slow down. Didn't want to slow down. Releasing a nipple with one last flick of his tongue over the hard tip, he continued his way down her body. He kissed and licked and nipped at her skin, loving the way she shivered and shook under his hands. When he reached her belly button, he swirled his tongue around it then pressed a kiss to the skin just below. He felt her stiffen, as if she'd just realized his intent. Not wanting to give her any time to think, he shoved his hands beneath her ass and lifted her hips.

His breath made the dark golden hair on her mound flutter, but it was her perfectly shaved pussy that held his undivided attention. The smooth, bare lips glistened, drawing his head down. His tongue flicked out to taste her, already knowing he'd love it. He swiped along the folds before stopping to tease her clit. She stilled as he devoured her, and he glanced up just to make sure she was still with him.

With her eyes closed and her head thrown back, she looked lost to desire. And with Rob still holding her hands above her head, she looked taken. She looked like she belonged to them.

She does.

With two fingers, he spread her lips, exposing her clit completely. She sucked in air, her back bowing off the bed, legs trying to close. Putting his hands on both thighs, he spread her wider and indulged himself. Every sound she made, every twist and turn of her body guided him, gave him more clues to unlocking her passion.

He sensed hesitancy from her, an unwillingness to give him everything, and he wasn't going to settle. He wanted it all. He wanted her to break apart in his hands and come on his tongue. Then he'd make her do it all over again when he got inside her.

Playing with her, tormenting her became the only thing he knew. He used his tongue on her until she was moaning under his hands, which slid up and her down her body, playing with her nipples or curving beneath her ass to shift her closer to his mouth.

He lost himself in the taste and feel of her, all his focus narrowed to one goal. To make her come.

It didn't take long to achieve. Seconds later, she stiffened, her hips snapping up, though his hands caught her before she could move more than a few centimeters. She breathed out his name as he worked his tongue inside her to feel the tight contractions of her pussy.

Damn, she'd be tight around his cock. He couldn't wait to feel her clutching at him.

Rising onto his knees, he shook his head to get his brain working again. And something landed next to him on the bed. Rob had released Ellie and tossed a condom onto the bed, within his reach. His gaze met Rob's for a split second, acknowledging his presence and the gift before Manny concentrated all his attention once again on Ellie.

She seemed to have to fight for every breath, but when her eyes opened, she stared at him with a look he couldn't misinterpret. And when she held out her arms, which Rob had released, he rolled the condom on and dropped down to kiss her. Hard. Fierce. Not giving her any leeway. She'd let him know she was his. He was holding her to it.

Her legs wrapped around his waist as he held himself above her on his elbows, his hips aligning his cock with her slit. He slid inside a centimeter at a time, not rushing although every brain cell was screaming at him to go faster, harder. To claim her.

When her arms wrapped around his shoulders and pulled him closer, he went, covering her completely with his body. Her sex gave way to his insistent cock, though he didn't thrust. He kept going slow and steady as he sank inside her. Until finally, he was completely immersed in her, her silky sheath clinging tightly to him.

When he couldn't go any farther, he held still, his gaze lost in hers. She looked up at him with lust. And a trust that made a pit grow in his stomach. If he wasn't careful, he'd get lost in those eyes. And he'd come without thrusting once.

No.

Dropping his mouth on hers, he kissed her hard, pulled his cock out until only the tip remained inside her heat. Then he thrust back in. Christ, she was hot. And tight. And wet.

His hips began to move in a slow rhythm, as slow as he could go. It was heaven, being inside her. And it was amazing to pull out and thrust again. And again. Until the motion became inescapable.

With her wrapped tight around him, her mouth pressed to his and their tongues entangled, he felt his orgasm build until he couldn't deny it any longer.

With a groan, he thrust deep and held, his cock pulsing with his release.

And his brain pounding with the realization that he didn't want to leave her.

SEVEN

Rob watched Ellie fall apart, his cock throbbing, blood blazing, and a knot in his gut that threatened to double him over.

He'd moved to a chair near the end of the bed when he'd released her. He was fairly sure they hadn't noticed. He'd seen everything. He'd watched Manny drive her crazy, watched her enjoy every damn second, and ignored his aching cock as best he could.

He'd almost unzipped his pants and jerked off while he watched but restrained himself. He wanted her to do it for him. And if she didn't... He could take care of himself later. He'd be fantasizing about this night for the foreseeable future so there'd be plenty of time.

Holy fuck, that'd been hot. He'd watched people have sex before. Hell, he got off on being an exhibitionist and this wasn't his first threesome.

But Manny had shocked the shit out of him. Rob had figured Manny would hesitate at being so exposed, even with Rob. They knew and trusted each other better than anyone else in the world, but Manny didn't like to expose himself. Not to anyone. This had come pretty damn close to exposing every-thing he held close. And Rob wasn't talking about Manny's bare ass.

And Ellie... Christ, he'd never expected Ellie to be...so uninhibited. His world seemed to have been flipped on its axis. He saw her in a totally different light and every muscle in his body ached from being restrained.

As he watched, Manny rolled onto his back, pulling Ellie with him. She ended up draped half on and half off his body, her eyes closed and her body limp, though she continued to breathe like she'd run a marathon.

Fuck.

He ground his back teeth, hands in fists, trying not to reach for her. Closing his eyes, he shook his head, telling himself he should leave. But dammit, he didn't want to fucking leave.

Don't be an asshole.

He slid to the edge of the chair and was just about to get up when Ellie opened her eyes and stared straight at him. She didn't look at all embarrassed. In fact, that look was a dare. She was daring him to...what? Leave? Join in?

He couldn't tell and that wasn't like him. Everything about this night was throwing him off.

Manny shifted, drawing Rob's attention, and he found Manny watching him. His best friend knew him well. He knew exactly what he was thinking. What he wanted. He also knew that Manny wasn't going to want to share her.

Manny turned his head to kiss Ellie, pulling her up the bed until their lips aligned. Ellie kissed him back, her hands rising to cup his jaw and hold him in place. Rob watched for several long seconds before he rose, fully intending to walk away.

"Rob."

Ellie's voice stopped him in his tracks, his back to the bed, jaw set.

He thought about continuing out the door without looking back, but he couldn't do it. He had to know what she wanted.

Turning, he put his hands in his pants' pockets, not trying to draw attention to his erection, but to keep his arms from crossing over his chest. He read body language like a pro. He didn't want to appear defensive.

And he couldn't stop his gaze from running down her naked body. Damn, she was beautiful. And not at all his type. He typically dated brunettes. Tanned, exotic, and with curves for days.

Ellie was peaches and cream, slight curves and wide blue eyes. The definition of girl next door...if the girl next door was an heiress who owned the company that employed you.

What could go wrong, right?

You're the one who likes a challenge, aren't you?

He lifted an eyebrow and waited for her to continue. If she wanted him to leave, he'd be out the door with a smile and a nod. Manny might be the only person on earth who'd know that smile would be fake.

He didn't say anything, just waited for her to continue. If she wanted him to stay, she had to ask. No way in hell would he stay where he wasn't wanted.

"Are you leaving?"

Grabbing a rumpled sheet, she pulled it up to her breasts, depriving him of the view he was enjoying immensely. With her hair messy and falling around her shoulders, and the toned-down makeup, she looked younger, sweeter. Innocent. Sexy.

He wanted to climb in bed, kiss his way up and down her body then curl around her and take her from behind. He couldn't tell from the tone of her voice if she was upset at the thought that he was leaving or relieved. He hoped to hell it wasn't the latter.

"Do you want me to leave?"

The look she gave him made him grin because it was such

an "Ellie" face. Part exasperation, part sweet amusement. But that smile also held a hint of heat. His body responded with a renewed surge of lust that he attempted to tamp down. And didn't do a very good job of it. That heat riled him up even more.

Fuck.

Then her brows rose, challenge clear on her face.

"Do you *want* to leave?"

Hell no. His gut tightened just thinking about it. But he didn't want her to think she had to invite him into her bed if she wasn't fully committed. He wanted her to fall apart in his arms as fully as she had in Manny's. He wanted nothing less.

"I'm not leaving. I'm going to run you a bath."

Her surprise was worth the ache in his cock.

"A bath?"

He nodded. "You haven't seen the bathroom yet. It'd be a shame if you don't spend at least an hour in the tub."

She stared at him for several long seconds, her expression inscrutable. Then her lips curved in a slight smile.

"Okay. That'd be nice."

Nodding, he headed for the bathroom, flipping on the light and walking to the tub.

He hadn't been exaggerating about the bathroom. She was going to love it. The freestanding whirlpool tub took up nearly half the room and could fit at least four people comfortably. It sat in front of the tinted window that looked out on the city.

The walls were covered in dark wood and the floors were marble, covered strategically with plush cotton rugs. The shower stall looked like it could fit five, boasting multiple showerheads. Hell, even the double sinks looked like you could bathe in them.

Walking to the tub, he flipped the lever and watched the water spill into it. Trying not to think. Seconds later, he heard movement behind him and turned to see Ellie, covered from head to toe in a white fluffy robe. He'd wondered if she'd turn shy now. Coy. Hell, maybe she'd be embarrassed.

Instead, she looked at the tub like a woman in love. His smile grew.

"Wow. Now, that is gorgeous."

Watching her walk forward, he could've said the same thing about her. If it'd been any other woman, he would have. Something made him bite his tongue on that one, knowing she would've dismissed it as another one of his lines. And maybe it would've been. But that didn't make it any less true.

"Any preference?"

He held up one of the many bottles on the edge. She looked at each one carefully before pointing to one.

He picked it up without looking at the label. When the liquid hit the water, the scent of coconut hit him. One of his favorites. Christ, he wanted to lather her body from head to toe with his hands. Would she let him?

A warning flashed through his brain. Tonight was turning out to be much more than he'd bargained for. And it wasn't over yet. He should've left before this got complicated. Because it was going to be fucking complicated. But he couldn't leave now. Didn't want to leave.

The tub filled rapidly, the bubbles almost to the rim, when he stood and gestured for her to come closer. She hesitated for a second, then closed the few feet between them. They were still alone. He didn't know if Manny had remained in bed or had dressed and left. He was betting on the first. Rob had a feeling Manny wanted to watch, too.

If there'd be anything to watch. Rob still wasn't sure there would be. They might've already pushed Ellie to her limit tonight. Then again, maybe he'd underestimated her.

He reached for the robe's sash, slowly, giving her time to

pull away. She watched his face as he worked the knot open. As the lapels fell apart, that grinding ache of desire churned in his gut. He'd seen her naked, yes. But the fact that she was only his in this moment made him greedy in a way he'd never been before.

He'd wanted women before, lusted after them. This felt different. He couldn't explain it and he sure as hell wasn't going to examine it too closely right now. But something about Ellie...

She continued to watch him, no hint of hesitation or embarrassment on her face as he pushed the robe off her shoulders. It slid to the floor, leaving her completely exposed.

Fuck, she was beautiful.

"This isn't fair."

Her voice held a husky rasp that stroked along his skin, making his muscles tense with desire and his cock harden until it was painfully stiff. Then her words registered. He shoved his hands in his pockets to keep from reaching out to cup her breasts and rub the dusky rose nipples into stiff peaks again.

"What do you mean?"

"I mean, I'm naked." She let her gaze slide down his body, lingering deliberately at his waist for several long seconds. "And you're not."

Her eyes locked with his again, challenging him.

The constraints he'd put on himself began to crumble away and his usual sense of fun emerged. He'd shoved it down and put it under lock to be able to keep himself in check earlier. He and Manny had few boundaries between them, but this was new. Ellie was an unknown element in their dynamic. He hadn't been sure how any of this would play out. How Ellie would react.

Hell, he wasn't sure how he'd been going to react.

"Do you want me to be naked?"

Her brows rose and that mouth he wanted to kiss for days pursed. "I think that's only fair, don't you?"

Then she stepped around him and climbed into the tub, sinking down into the bubbles until she was completely covered, except for her head and shoulders.

"Mmm, coconut." Her eyes fluttered closed as she took a deep breath. "I love this scent."

He had a feeling he was never going to be able to smell it and not think of her.

Movement behind him caught his attention, and he turned to see Manny leaning against the doorjamb. He'd put on his pants, but nothing else.

Rob grinned. Okay, now they were getting somewhere.

Turning back to Ellie, looking up at him from the tub, he unbuttoned his shirt and tossed it on the floor, followed by his pants, underwear, and socks. He'd taken his shoes off in the other room.

Then, as she laughed, he climbed into the other end of the tub.

"Damn, this thing is almost too big. Never thought I'd say that about anything."

Her eyes widened and her lips parted at the purposeful double entendre, which just gave him time to reach over and slide her closer.

Cupping her face in his hands, he put his mouth on her and kissed her. Like he'd been dreaming about for the past few days. She didn't hesitate. She gave him what he wanted. Everything. Immediately.

His tongue slid past her lips and tangled with hers, going from zero to heart attack in a second. Probably because he'd already been primed and ready to go. Spreading his legs, he drew her into his body until her drawn-up knees were only inches away from his chest. She kissed him back with an experience he hadn't expected and that enflamed his already burning lust.

His fingers slid into her hair, tilting her head so he could get a better angle, kiss her even deeper. She reached for him, settling her hands on his shoulders and leaning forward.

It'd be so easy to drape her legs over his hips and pull her forward until he could settle her on his cock. He had to swallow a groan just thinking about it. He didn't want to rush, but sometimes rushing was exactly what you needed. What he needed.

His hands slid down to her shoulders then carefully bypassed her breasts to skim down to her hips and her thighs. She sighed into his mouth as his fingers pressed against her skin, curling around her thighs and tugging her closer.

He felt her suck in air, felt her stiffen beneath his hands for a second then wiggle even closer. When he lifted her legs to drape them over his thighs, she leaned back to help. And when he had her situated, she surprised the hell out of him and plastered her body against him. Her arms tightened around his shoulders as her breasts pressed against his chest. The lush softness of her body made his arms tighten around her waist, made his lips demand more. Made his cock throb with a lust he'd never imagined he could feel for this woman

For that matter, he'd never imagined Ellie would respond to him like this. Like she was dying for him to fuck her. She'd never looked at him like other women did, with lust. He'd honestly thought she didn't like him. At least, she'd never looked at him like she'd wanted to kiss him the way she was now.

She was practically crawling on top of him, which would've turned him off if he hadn't wanted her just as badly.

He wanted to settle her on his cock and rock them both into an orgasm she wouldn't forget. And leave her begging for more.

His erection continued to harden until his balls fucking ached. It took every ounce of his control not to lift her hips and slide inside her. But that control was fading fast. Every breathy sound she made as she kissed him, every time she tilted her head a little more to give him a better angle to kiss her, every time her fingers clenched into his shoulders as she pressed her breasts even tighter against his chest, pushed him closer to the edge.

Typically, he liked to take his time with a woman. Play around. Drive her a little crazy.

If he wasn't careful, he was going to be the one begging.

At the moment, he wouldn't care.

His arms tightened around her waist, pulling her even closer. He felt her mound press against his cock, heard her moan deep in her chest. Then she moved even closer and angled her body up.

He knew what she wanted. Exactly what he did.

Breaking the seal with her lips proved harder than he'd expected. He didn't want to stop now that he had her exactly where he wanted her. But he needed a condom. He'd stayed at Haven countless times. The rooms were stocked with everything you could want.

What he needed was either in a drawer by the sink or—

He pulled away to glance around the tub and found what he was looking for in the alcove. A waterproof box within easy reach. Trust Jared Golden to think of the most accessible place for condoms near the tub.

Flipping open the box, he grabbed a condom then looked back to find Ellie watching his every move. He'd wondered if she'd start to second guess now, but her expression showed only excitement.

A flare of emotion licked around his chest, catching him off guard, and nearly tipped him off balance. Sex had nothing to do with emotion. That's how he'd always functioned. Sex was fun, companionship. It didn't mean anything more. He'd watched his father fuck his way around Hollywood even while swearing his undying devotion to his wife, who'd never seemed to have a problem with her husband's infidelity. Probably because she'd had her own affairs.

Considering they were still married and seemed to be happy, Rob had come to an early conclusion that love and sex were two totally different things.

This was sex. Yeah, he'd lusted after this woman for years, but that was sex. He didn't want to spend the rest of his life with her. Didn't want to be tied to one woman forever. He just didn't think he had it in him.

When... No, *if* he ever decided to settle down, it'd be with a woman who knew the score. Someone with the same ideals.

Yeah, someone who doesn't love you enough to care who you sleep with.

Ellie deserved someone like Manny, who'd love her completely. That's why Rob was going to enjoy the hell out of tonight, because he was pretty sure it would *never* happen again.

His gaze snapped to the door, where he'd last seen Manny. Who wasn't there. Where the hell would he have gone?

There. Rob found him in the mirror, sitting on the upholstered bench across the room, his attention fixed on Ellie. Rob didn't look too closely but he was pretty sure the guy had a hard-on. How could he not? Rob certainly had while he'd watched Manny and Ellie.

Time to return the favor.

Tearing open the packet, he sank his hands beneath the water and rolled it on. Ellie's hands followed his but popped up again when she realized the bubbles hid what he was doing. Her smile had a playful edge to it, an expression he'd never seen on her face before.

That would become pretty fucking addictive if he let it. Which he couldn't.

"Do you need help?"

The tease in her voice and the nearness of her mouth made the pit in his stomach widen. He'd never expected her to be so... playful. Frankly, he hadn't known what to expect.

Not gonna happen.

"I think I can manage."

"Are you sure?"

"Ellie, if you want to put your hands on me, you don't need to ask for permission."

He watched her smile fade even as the glint in her eyes sharpened.

"Is that an invitation?"

"Do you need one?"

A second later, one of her hands began to trail down his chest. When it disappeared beneath the bubbles, he felt her fingers trail the length of his cock. He bit back a groan as she scraped her nails along his balls, making his erection rock-hard.

Her lips twitched at the corners, and that pit in his stomach became an all-consuming ache. Had he been blind these past few years? Yes, he'd noticed how beautiful she was, but he hadn't realized how sexy. He didn't think he'd forget it any time soon.

That's gonna lead to issues.

Fuck it. It wasn't an issue now as she wrapped her hand around his cock and started to pump. His breathing shallowed out as their gazes held. She stroked him with a tight, steady grip that fired his lust and burned out any rational thought. Instinct took over, like acid drop-loaded into his bloodstream. He lifted her hips, watching her eyes narrow to slits.

"Wrap your legs around my waist, Ellie. Let's soak the floor."

Her smile curved a second before he sealed their mouths together. Her legs curved around his hips and tightened as she arched her back and her hands tilted his cock at the right angle to lodge at the entrance to her sex.

He didn't forge ahead. Not yet. He let the anticipation build, his cock throbbing with it. Her breathing deepened, her arm encircling his shoulders, pulling him closer.

Holy fuck. He wasn't sure he wouldn't come as soon as he got inside her. But he couldn't wait any longer. His fingers flexed on her hips, drawing her closer. His cock spread her lips, sinking deeper, the tightness of her sheath attempting to blow his mind with each inch he gained. He took it as slow as he could, wanting to draw this out. But when she wiggled her hips and took him all the way in, he groaned and pulled her down, completely encased inside her.

Water sloshed around them, the motion of the water against his skin another sensual trigger. He loved being in the water, loved to surf and swim. Hell, he loved any sport that took place in the water. Guess he could add sex to the list now.

You've had sex in water before.

But he'd never had sex with Ellie before. And sex in water with Ellie was knocking him off his axis. She threatened to make him lose his control, to overwhelm his senses. It was an unfamiliar feeling, and he felt himself fighting against it.

He didn't want to lose himself in this girl. *Couldn't* lose himself in this girl. She wasn't his.

Will never be yours.

Didn't mean he couldn't have fun now. Especially when he felt her straining to get closer, her lips moving over his with a hunger that stoked his lust.

Weaving the fingers of one hand through her hair, he

gripped her hip with the other and pulled her even closer. She didn't wait for any more direction. She took over.

Rocking against him, she set the pace. Slow at first, so fucking slow he felt every centimeter of her sex as she gripped him. When the tip of his cock threatened to escape, she arched her hips and slid back down.

After long, long seconds of steady pacing, she slid forward then held again. The hand he'd had on her hip flattened on her belly, his thumb finding her clit and pressing against it. She released his mouth with a gasp, her forehead falling into the curve of his neck and shoulder. Her breath rushed against his skin, his cock responding with an almost painful throb. He could feel the effort it was taking her to hold still while he teased her. Almost as if she felt he'd stop if she moved.

"Come on, Ellie. Move."

She sucked in air, her sheath tightening around him. "Feels good."

"It'll feel better when you move."

Her hands gripped his shoulders again as she took him, careful not to dislodge his thumb. When her breath started to come hard and fast and her movements became less smooth, he increased the pressure on her clit. He wanted her to come first, wanted her clenching around him when he hit his own peak.

Continuing to play with her, he moved his free hand to her ass to steady her and to add a little force to her downward thrusts. She took the hint and rocked harder, until the water roiled around them. He felt his orgasm approaching, felt his balls tighten and his breaths get short and choppy. But she wasn't there yet.

So he moved the hand on her ass to the soft, soft skin between her cheeks, which made her falter for several seconds. She didn't stop, but he felt her anticipation, for whatever he was going to do next.

Using only his index finger, he traced a line to the tiny pucker of her ass. Now she stopped completely, holding steady. Waiting for him. When he stroked the sensitive skin around that entrance, she shuddered, but not in fear or distaste. She wanted more. He gave it to her.

Making sure he didn't hurt her, he massaged the skin as he started to move. She didn't protest when he removed his thumb from her clit, wrapping that arm around her waist so he could maneuver better. Now he took over the rhythm, teasing that little hole and the sensitive skin around it until he heard her practically panting.

And when he finally pierced that entrance with his finger, she moaned, cupping his jaw in both hands and kissing him with wild abandon. And blasting through the last bit of his control.

He fucked her hard and fast then, his finger thrusting in opposition to his cock.

He broke first, with a groan that rumbled through his chest and into her mouth. His cock pulsed with his release and a second later, she stiffened and held as he felt her contract, squeezing every last drop out of him.

Long seconds later, she released his mouth and tucked her head under his chin, breathing heavily against his chest. His heart pounded so hard he knew she had to hear it.

Rob held Ellie against him with tight arms, his brain already trying to work out what the hell had happened. He'd lost himself in her, and that was something he'd never done. Sex wasn't love. Sex was fun. And no ties. Never any ties.

Right now, it felt a hell of a lot like she'd wrapped a whole hell of a lot of strings around him and was tying him to her.

He needed to take a mental step back. Needed space. And couldn't find it.

Holy. Fuck. He and Manny were in a fuck-ton of trouble.

ELLIE HAD the sudden realization that she didn't know how to leave this room in any way that wasn't awkward.

Rob had kissed her cheek, settled her on the other side of the tub, then gotten out. He'd dried off, wrapped a towel around his waist, and disappeared into the other room. Manny had exchanged a look with Rob as he left, then Manny grabbed a towel and walked it over to the tub.

Without a word, he'd held out his hand, helped her out, wrapped her in fluffy cotton and opened his mouth to speak. Then he seemed to think better of it, nodded, and left.

So here she sat, alone, wrapped in a towel—Oh wait. Her clothes sat on the bench on the far wall. Manny must've brought them in after she'd come around Rob's cock and was still floating in a post-orgasmic state.

Ooh-kay.

Probably past time to get the hell out of here.

Luckily, the bathroom was stocked with anything she could need. Comb, hair ties, body lotion, deodorant. Maybe she could just live here until Rob and Manny went away.

Suck it up, buttercup. Yeah, you just had sex with two men. You're a grown-ass adult. Act like it.

She could do this. The more seconds passed, the more urgent her need to leave became, until it was a beat in the back of her skull, like a ticking clock. By the time she was dressed and had her hand on the doorknob, she realized there was no easy way to do this. So she put on a smile and walked into the bedroom.

And came to a stop after only a few feet.

Manny and Rob stared at each other, their expressions tight. She had the feeling they'd been arguing. She had no idea about what but that just made getting out of here that much more imperative. She needed peace and quiet to work her head around what had happened.

Sucking in a breath, she thought about what she should say but couldn't think of a damn thing besides, "Have you seen my shoes?"

Manny's gaze narrowed as if she'd just asked him to fly naked on a broom.

"Next to the bed," Rob said.

And so they were. Next to the bed that looked like someone had spent a restless night in them. Or had their brains fucked out of them. Now she really needed to get out of here.

Slipping on her shoes, she grabbed her purse from the chair where she'd dropped it earlier. Then she stiffened her backbone and walked over to face them.

Manny's gaze had narrowed, watching her every move like a hawk, trying to dissect her. Rob looked at her as if she came bearing a bomb.

"Thank you for tonight." It was the only thing she could think to say that wasn't literally thanking them for fucking her. "I...guess I'll see you at the office."

She wanted the floor to swallow her. How stupid could she sound? Seriously, she just needed to leave.

"If you're ready, we can drive you home."

"That's not necessary. I'm going to take a taxi."

Manny did not like that, at all. He wanted to argue, his lips parted to speak, when Rob put his hand on Manny's arm. Just for a second, and if you blinked you would've missed it, but she'd seen.

"I'll call down and have one waiting for you."

She exchanged a look with Rob and couldn't tell if he was just as anxious to be rid of her as she was to leave. Or if he wanted to head off a confrontation. Or maybe he realized she was hanging on to her calm by a thread.

Whatever the reason, she was grateful for the assist.

She had the door open when Manny finally spoke up.

"We'll talk tomorrow, Ellie."

She fled like the clock was striking twelve and she was about to turn back into a pumpkin.

EIGHT

"Wow. By the looks of you, I'm guessing your date went well. Or really bad. Are you okay? You look kinda..."

Brianna stood at Ellie's door Monday morning at the ungodly hour of six a.m. Ellie probably should've canceled their weekly date for yoga and breakfast before work, but honestly, she'd forgotten about it until her alarm had gone off this morning.

Of course, then she was awake, and she knew she wouldn't be going back to sleep because her brain had started to churn. Hopefully yoga would help her find her balance this morning. Because last night had blown it to pieces.

Ellie mumbled something that sounded like good morning as she grabbed her yoga bag from the chair by the door, prepared to power through sixty-five minutes of contorting her body in ways that defied logic.

But Brianna didn't move out of the doorway.

"Ellie? Ahh... Are you sure you wanna go like that?"

"Like what?"

Brianna's eyes widened then she pointedly looked down at Ellie's feet. Her gaze followed. To her bare feet.

"Well, shit." Ellie sighed, shaking her head as she waved Brianna through the door. "Give me a minute."

"You know what? Why don't we take a whole hour and just skip yoga?" Brianna suggested. "And then you can tell me all about last night."

Ellie yawned, her jaw cracking with the strength of it. "Yeah, that might be the smart thing to do. I probably would've spent the entire class in savasana anyway. Good thing I had groceries delivered yesterday. You want blueberry or strawberry Pop-Tarts?"

"Ooh, it's a Pop-Tart day." Brianna's tone immediately perked up. "Now I'm really interested in what happened last night. Spill."

"Coffee first. If I start talking now, it might not make any sense."

Of course, it probably wasn't going to make a hell of a lot of sense anyway because her mind and her heart had been confusing issues since she'd left the guys in that hotel room and fled for the relative safety of her apartment.

In seconds, she and Brianna were settled at the breakfast bar with coffee and the sweets she only allowed herself to eat once or twice a month because they were so damn addictive. Like she feared Manny and Rob were going to be.

Ten minutes later, Ellie was properly medicated with coffee and sugar and ready to attempt to analyze her issues.

Propping her chin on her hand, she wrinkled her nose at Brianna. "I'm afraid I might be in over my head."

Brianna put on her serious face, about to put her human behavioral degree to use. "Tell me what you mean by that."

"I mean, I'm not sure I should've gone last night."

"Why?"

"Because I don't know if this is going to work."

"You've lost me." Brianna shook her head. "What won't work?"

"This thing between Rob and Manny and me."

Eyes wide, Brianna bit her bottom lip before saying, "I didn't know it was a thing. Or that you wanted it to be. I thought you said you just wanted no-strings sex."

Ellie had thought she had an answer to that, but when she considered one now, she couldn't come up with anything that sounded reasonable. Or plausible. Or sane.

"I did. I do! I just..."

Just what?

"Ellie. We all know you've had the hots for Manny since you were a kid." Brianna made it sound like it was the common knowledge. And maybe it was. "But I thought you didn't like Rob. That must have been some damn good sex to make you want to hook up with the guy again."

"I don't hate Rob. I just...never considered him boyfriend material. I mean, I still don't consider him boyfriend material. He's just..."

Brianna's head cocked to the side. "Just what?"

"Not what I expected."

"How so?"

"I mean, he's different when we were...alone."

Brianna made a face her friends considered her "royally vexed" face. "I think you're going to need to explain this to me."

"I don't know if I can because I'm not sure I understand it myself."

Brianna's expression went soft, and her smile made Ellie sigh in frustration.

"You like him." Brianna's tone held an excitement Ellie needed to nip in the bud.

"I never said I didn't like him." Ellie's lip curled at the mulishness in her voice. "Fine. I guess maybe I had preconceived notions that turned out to be wrong. Or maybe he was just being nice to me because we were having sex. Hell, I don't know what to think anymore."

Brianna dismissed that with a shrug of her shoulder. "I don't think Rob's that kind of guy. I think he likes you."

"You make it sound like we're in high school."

Brianna's brows rose. "The situation kinda sounds like it. Except for the fact that you had sex. With both of them. I'm assuming the sex was good?"

Ellie sighed. She couldn't help it. "Yes, the sex was good. Great. Okay, it was amazing. I want more. From both of them. But I don't know what they want. I mean, I don't know if we're ever going to repeat last night."

"What did they say afterward?"

"I didn't give them a chance to say anything. I got dressed, basically told them 'Hey, thanks for the orgasm,' and ran. I took a taxi home. I'm pretty sure Manny nearly had a brain aneurysm when I left. And now I have to go to work and run into them in the halls and pretend like nothing happened. I don't know how I'm supposed to face them. I mean, do I act like it was no big deal? Like, 'Hey, we had sex. Have a great day.' I'm just not sure what happens now."

"Don't you think you should talk to them before you decide they don't want a repeat performance?"

"Of course. I just don't know what to say."

"Just tell them the truth."

"And what if I don't know what that is?"

Brianna gave her that look, the one that made it clear Ellie knew exactly what she should say. Ellie wrinkled her nose and stuck her tongue out at Brianna.

Brianna, damn her, just laughed. "I'm sorry. I don't mean to make fun. But you have to admit your tune certainly has changed."

"I know. I just don't know what I'm going to do about it."

"I say you should do what you want."

If only it were that easy. "And what if I want something they don't?"

"You're only going to know if you talk to them. People definitely need to talk more."

There was something in Brianna's voice that made Ellie take a good look at her. She'd been so wrapped up in her own issues that she hadn't realized something was going on with her friend.

"Bri? Is something wrong?"

Brianna shook her head, a little too vehemently. "No. Of course not. Tell me—"

"Bri. Stop. What happened?"

Brianna's nose crinkled, but she wouldn't meet Ellie's gaze head-on. "Why do you think something happened?"

"Because you're trying to act like nothing happened."

"Nothing happened." She sighed. "I mean, it's just..." Huge sigh. "My parents want me to come home. They didn't come right out and say that but..." Shrugging, she shook her head. "I was a late baby. They're getting older. I'm their only child. If I don't agree to come home in the next year, they're going to appoint a successor."

Though she didn't publicize the fact, Brianna was an actual princess of a tiny principality in Europe. Smaller than Monaco and hidden away in the Alps, Arrora had a population of maybe five thousand people, and most everyone who lived there made it their life's pursuit to remain under the radar. Brianna was more than happy to pretend to be just another European studying in America with an accent that no one could quite place.

Except her dad was amazingly good at making money. Everything he touched turned to gold. Not literally, of course, but the man was worth hundreds of millions of dollars, which made Brianna the occasional target of European tabloids. Which was why she lived in the states under an assumed name and was careful not to let anyone know who and what she really was.

But while her parents had sent her to the US for her education when she was fourteen, they'd started making comments referencing her returning home about a year ago. Basically, they wanted her to give up everything she'd built here and run their country. So far, Brianna had put them off by continuing her education. But it looked like that excuse wasn't going to fly much longer.

"Do you want to go home?"

Brianna looked torn and a little heartbroken. "Someday."

The way she said that gave Ellie the impression Brianna's timetable didn't mesh with her parents'.

"Be honest." Ellie reached over to take Brianna's hand. "Do you want to lead Arrora?"

With a huff, Brianna shook her head. "I thought maybe I would, when I got older. But I'm older and... I don't think I want to give up my entire life for my country. I'm a horrible person, aren't I?"

"No, of course you're not. You have your own dreams. That's not a bad thing."

"It is if your dream is to be a high school counselor and help teenagers get through the roughest years of their lives. I just want to have a normal life."

"Are you sure you just don't want to lead an entire country, and this is your way of avoiding that?"

Brianna squeezed her hand, her smile turning wry. "I hate that you're so smart. And I love you to pieces."

Ellie rose and headed for the cabinet. "I think this calls for more Pop-tarts. And hey, it's not like your parents don't have someone who can run the country, right? I mean, there have to be other family members who can step up."

"Of course." Brianna's expression had dimmed, but now she pushed all that gloom aside and smiled. "Now, what are *you* going to do about Manny and Rob?"

Of course, they would come back to that.

"Honestly, I don't have a clue. But I think I'm going to avoid the situation completely and not go into the office today. Wanna play hooky with me?"

"WHERE THE HELL have you been all day? We need to talk."

Rob looked up at Manny, standing in the door to his office late Monday afternoon. He'd been hoping like hell he could avoid this conversation, at least until Wednesday. He had that fucking photo shoot with his family tomorrow, and between that and last night, he'd been avoiding the hell out of everything and everyone.

"I've had meetings all day. What do you need?"

Manny just stared at him, because of course he knew what they needed to talk about. Which was exactly what Rob didn't want to talk about. So he'd made sure he was out of the building.

Walking into his office, Manny shut the door behind him. Probably a good call. Didn't want Jack to accidentally hear what they'd done to his goddaughter last night. They'd both be out on their asses.

Manny's arms crossed over his chest, his stare level. "How were your meetings?"

Okay, sure, Rob could play this game. "The meetings went fine. And your day?"

"Spent most of it wondering when we're going to talk about Ellie."

Fucking Manny and his one-track mind. Rob leaned back in his chair and returned Manny's gaze.

"Nothing to talk about." Rob shook his head, making sure his expression stayed neutral. *Nothing to see here, folks.* "Last night was a one-off."

Manny's brows lifted, just enough to make Rob's back teeth grind. "You really believe that?"

Rob had to make a conscious effort to loosen his jaw. "That was the arrangement. Or did I miss something?"

"I don't remember there being a time limit attached to our arrangement."

"And I don't remember Ellie asking us to make more plans."

Manny's lips twitched. "I think we gave her too many orgasms to think straight. I think if we ask her out again, she'll say yes."

Fuck. That just made him remember her coming around his cock buried deep inside her. He'd been trying not to think too hard about that; otherwise, he wouldn't think about anything else.

"Then go ahead. I'll be out of town tomorrow anyway for that photo shoot."

Manny fell silent and let it drag out, just staring as if he could change Rob's mind by looking at him.

Bastard.

"Damn it." Rob broke after only a couple of seconds, knowing Manny wasn't going to let this go. "She's not going to miss me. I was just a bonus cock. A little variety, for fuck's sake. We both know she's hung up on you."

Manny's brows rose about a millimeter, just enough for Rob's teeth to set again. At the rate he was going, he'd have his molars ground into dust in no time.

"Sounds like you're jealous."

"I'm not fucking jealous." Definitely an edge to Rob's voice now. He swore he could feel it. "I'm just not willing to be a fuck toy for a spoiled heiress."

Manny's expression didn't change, but Rob knew he'd pushed too far. Hell, he hadn't even meant it. That's not what he thought of Ellie. Wasn't even close to what he thought about her. He knew why he'd said it, though. Because he was right about one thing.

She wasn't interested in him as anything other than a bed partner. She wanted Manny. Rob had simply been a bonus. Whitney's relationship with Chase and Ryan had made Ellie curious. Curious enough to include Rob in last night's activities. But he couldn't believe it was enough for her to consider giving a three-way relationship a try.

Coward.

Fuck that. He wasn't a coward. He was a pragmatist. Which was usually Manny's job.

Shit.

"You're being an asshole." It was a wonder Manny could get the words through his teeth. "She doesn't deserve that."

No, she didn't, but if it got Manny off the damn subject, he'd play the asshole. "Then it's a good thing I'm taking myself out of the picture."

The muscles in Manny's jaw jumped. "I'm going to ask her out again for Thursday."

"Good. I'm sure you'll have a great time."

"What the fuck are you so afraid of?"

Rob generally thought of himself as a pretty reasonable guy, not quick to anger. But Manny knew what buttons to push.

"Maybe I just don't want her as much as you do."

"Bullshit." Manny's answer was quick and sure. "That's not what I saw last night. Don't you realize, we can give her more pleasure than she could ever imagine. She can be ours."

The emotion that punched Rob in the gut was unexpected.

Because he wanted her to be theirs. More than he'd ever thought he would. More than he should because it wasn't going to happen.

"It won't work."

Manny sighed hard. "Why are you so hell-bent against this?"

"Maybe because I'm not in love with her and you are."

"No one's talking about love. Except you. Why is that?"

"For fuck's sake, I'm not talking about love. I'm stating a fact, which you're conveniently throwing back in my face. Why can't you admit your feelings for her? Why are you so much more interested in mine?"

"Because I'm fucking worried about you."

Manny's even tone with just a hint of tension was a low blow against Rob's defenses. He hadn't been prepared for it, and he certainly hadn't expected it.

"What? Why?"

"Because I'm watching you devolve back into that asshole I first met at school, and I fucking hate it. What the fuck is going on with you?"

Another blow, this one landing even harder. Because Manny wasn't wrong. He'd felt it himself, felt him losing the man he'd made himself into. Why? Did he even know?

Manny stared at him, waiting, dark gaze boring into him.

"I don't know." Rob shook his head, his answer as true as he could make it. "I'm not sure it's something that can be fixed. Or that I need to fix. It might just be me."

"No." Manny shook his head. "This isn't you. The faster you realize that, the better."

"Maybe I need space. Maybe I've decided it's time to move on. Maybe I'm just ready for something different."

A muscle in Manny's jaw started to twitch, a sure sign Rob was pushing him too hard. But, dammit, Rob felt the same. He had too much shit in his head right now. His mom's run for office was going to require him to be on display, but he wasn't sure how long he could put up with his dad before they began trading barbs. His sister would be living practically next door, which should've made him ecstatic. He'd been pushing for her to move east for years. And now that she had, he wanted to run. He felt like the walls were closing in on him.

What the fuck was wrong with him?

"And maybe shit's just getting too real for you."

Manny's barb stung.

"Maybe you need to look at the skeletons in your own damn closet. Ask yourself why you don't want to pursue her on your own."

Manny shrugged, visibly unfazed by Rob's jab. "Maybe. But I'm not the one who's running."

"ELLIE. CAN WE TALK?"

Ellie's feet froze to the floor outside her classroom at the institute Tuesday night. She'd just finished teaching her last class for the day, the four-to-five-year-old Intro to Ballet. Her favorite, if she had to pick. The kids were a joy. High energy, giggly, and adorable. Even if they threw a tantrum, she couldn't get over how stinking cute they were.

Of course, she had the luxury of sending them home after forty-five minutes, but still.

So she'd been smiling as she walked the last child out of the classroom, a little girl whose mom always ran late because of work. Ellie didn't mind. She had nothing to do tonight, and Maisie was a joy. From the top of her pigtailed head to the tiny pink ballet slippers on her feet, the little girl who spoke a mix of Spanish and English always had an interesting story.

Tonight, the story had been about her brother, Michal, a young teenager who took Ellie's intermediate ballet class Monday, Wednesday, and Friday. The boy had the skill to become a professional dancer, but Ellie was afraid she was losing him. He'd become more withdrawn the last couple of months as school approached and he headed to junior high. She lost so many of her promising boys when they hit that age, it was heartbreaking.

But right now, her heart wasn't breaking. It was threatening to beat out of her chest because Manny stood in the hall, next to the one-way mirror that allowed parents to watch.

A tug on her hand had her looking down. "Miss Perrault. He's a big man. Should I call for help?"

The look on Manny's face was priceless as Ellie's smile widened as she bent down to talk to the little girl.

"No, this is my friend, Mr. Bianchi." She glanced up at Manny. "Mr. Bianchi, this is Maisie."

Maisie, for all that she was five, was also a Philly girl. She looked Manny up and down through narrowed dark eyes. "He looks too old to be your friend."

Ellie glanced at Manny again and caught his mouth quirking into a devastating grin. Then he held his hand out and Ellie nearly melted into a puddle of goo.

"How do you do, Miss Maisie?"

Maisie wasn't as charmed. She took his hand, but only for a second and scrunched up her face. "I do ballet. What do you do?"

"I..." Manny searched for words, obviously wanting to find the right ones for the little girl who looked at him so suspiciously, "protect people and their businesses."

"So you're a cop?" Maisie didn't sound like she approved of that.

"I'm more like a firefighter."

Ellie smiled at his analogy, knowing exactly why he'd used it. Manny put out fires and protected the assets of the company, whether they were people or intellectual property. Maisie apparently thought that was okay. Her lips loosened and curved into a little bit of a smile.

"I like fire trucks. They make noise. I like noise. Michal!"

Maisie released Ellie's hand and took off down the hall to her brother, stopping only to wave good-bye to Ellie and Manny. Michal inclined his head but didn't get close enough for Ellie to speak to him. She'd have to save that for another day.

Because Manny had tracked her down and she was dying to know why. Neither Manny or Rob had contacted her Monday or today. No text. No call. Nothing. Of course, she hadn't contacted them, either.

No one had mentioned a future date Sunday night. Not even a "Hey, thanks for the great sex, let's do it again sometime." She hadn't known what to expect, but it hadn't been radio silence.

Of course, she'd practically run out of the hotel room like her ass was on fire, so she could understand why they might've been a little put off.

Except, here was Manny. Only Manny.

"I think I was just put on notice by a toddler."

Ellie laughed at Manny's dry statement, entranced by the glint in his eyes and the hint of a grin on his lips. Lips that had kissed most of her body Sunday night.

She swallowed hard, lust making her burn from the inside out. Her cheeks were going to give away her any second now, but she didn't care. She'd allowed this man intimate access and she'd give it to him again. Now. In an hour. Whenever he wanted. Because holy crap, that night had been freaking amazing.

It'd taken her all day to realize she'd run the night before last because she's been afraid. Afraid of what could happen if she let herself dream. Let herself hope. But she'd realized during her Advanced Pointe class, as she'd been coaching a student through a particularly difficult step, that she wasn't taking her own advice.

"Don't try it. Do it. Then decide if you want to do it again."

She'd done it. She wanted to do it again. But Manny was here alone.

"I think Maisie's superpower is to tie men around her finger. You're just the latest in a long line, trust me."

He nodded and she was pretty sure he was responding to her comment about Maisie. Then his gaze sharpened.

"You weren't in the office yesterday."

"No, I took the day off with Brianna. She's having some personal issues." Not a lie. At least, not completely. "We did retail therapy."

Manny nodded, as if he took her statement at face value. "Come out with me tonight."

Her heart stuttered in her chest, excitement ricocheting like a bullet in a steel box. She tried not to act like a teenager being asked to the prom but wasn't sure she pulled it off.

"I'd like that. Will...Rob be joining us too?"

Manny's jaw clenched and she kicked herself for asking.

"No. He's in Maryland for a photo shoot with his family."

Manny didn't sound thrilled about that, which made sense, considering the little she knew about Rob's relationship with his dad.

She smiled at him. "I'd love to go out tonight."

"Are you ready to leave now?"

She huffed out a laugh and waved a hand down her body.

"I'm not exactly dressed to go out."

"I think you look beautiful."

Her eyes widened as she looked down at herself. White

tights, scuffed ballet slippers, see-through wrap skirt, and short-sleeve pink leotard. Her hair was pulled back in a bun and she wore no makeup.

"Thank you. But I really do need to change."

"If we get takeout and go back to my place, do you still need to change?"

She only had to look at his face to realize he was completely serious. Her heart twinged and her lungs felt heavy, like the air had gotten thicker and harder to breathe.

"No. I guess...I don't."

"What do you want to eat?"

She didn't care, as long as she ate it with him. Hell, they could skip food completely and go straight for dessert, and she didn't mean chocolate, unless it was syrup that she licked off his body.

Now her cheeks burned, and the air was not only heavy but hot. And her sex tightened and ached.

"I don't really have a craving for anything." Liar. "Whatever you want is fine."

His grin hinted that he knew her secret, that she was dying for another taste of him.

"I know the perfect place."

Half an hour later, they sat at the dining table in his home. She was eating the best Cobb salad she'd ever had in her life and Manny had devoured a slab of meatloaf that could've fed her for three meals.

"I can't believe I've never heard of that diner before. Their food is amazing."

"I discovered it a few months ago after a meeting went late. It was the only place open in the vicinity and I was starving. I've been back at least five times since then."

"It's not that far from my apartment. I'll definitely be going back."

"I'm sure Georgie will love that. She liked you. It took at least three times before she warmed up to me."

"I don't believe that." Ellie shook her head as she pushed her plate away from her. "Georgie seemed more than happy to see you."

And he had seemed comfortable there. Not that he wasn't comfortable here or at the office, but there'd just been something...easier about him there.

"She's a good person. And her wife. Hard to find decent people in the world anymore."

"That sounds cynical."

Shrugging, he picked up their plates and took them to the sink. They'd eaten in the kitchen, at a small round table, instead of the formal dining room she'd noticed on their way to the kitchen. She hadn't known what to expect, but she'd fallen in love with his home at first sight. She thought her condo was great, but this place... She hadn't expected him to live in a beautiful old row home in Rittenhouse Square. The architectural details were amazing, from the wood trim to the pocket doors and the original wood-burning fireplaces in practically every room.

She'd been expecting something more modern. Stripped down. This place was none of those things.

"I guess. But I'm not wrong."

"I like to think there are more good people than bad." She paused, thought for a second. "You think I'm naïve, don't you?"

He walked back to the table, grabbed his chair and turned it backward so he could rest his arms on the back as he sat next to her.

"I think you have a good heart. I'd hate to see you hurt."

Her breath caught as she turned in her chair to face him. Was she supposed to read something into that statement? Was he telling her not to get attached to him because he'd hurt her?

He held her gaze, and the urge to kiss him became a pounding drumbeat in her chest. All she had to do was lean forward and he'd get the hint. He'd kiss her like she wanted to be kissed.

Then again, why wait for what she wanted?

Leaning forward, she pressed her mouth to his, let her lips meld to his. He responded immediately, much to her delight. His head tilted and his hands came up to cup the back of her head and urge her even closer.

As her arms wound around his shoulders, her tongue licked at the seam of his lips. Her stomach knotted when he groaned deep in his throat and he opened to her, letting her in. She kissed him for long seconds, letting their tongues tangle and her desire for him grow until it felt like a beast she couldn't contain within her skin any longer.

She wanted to climb all over him, but the chair situation was totally not working in her favor. Frustrated, she pulled back and huffed, eyes narrowing as she considered the situation.

Manny's smile made her swoon. She literally felt light-headed, although that could just be the fact that she couldn't seem to catch her breath.

"Problem?"

The amusement in his voice made her eyes narrow as she looked at him.

"As a matter of fact, yes."

She stood and started walking toward the living room and the large sectional sofa she'd seen there. He appeared to be in the mood to play, and she was going to take advantage of every second he gave her because she wasn't sure when she'd have him to herself again. If she'd have him again. Which she did not want to think about now. Or the fact that there was a little part of her that was disappointed Rob wasn't here.

She shoved that feeling away before Manny picked up on it.

Rob had a family obligation. He wasn't deliberately snubbing her. Although she wasn't sure he would've shown up anyway. She wasn't sure about anything after Sunday night. She felt like she'd gotten knocked off the merry-go-round she'd been riding but was still spinning.

Behind her, she heard Manny moving then his quiet footsteps as he followed her. It became harder for her to breathe, feeling like she was being stalked. She liked it. Strange but true.

At the couch, she made a move to turn, but Manny wrapped his arms around her waist and dragged her back against his front. His erection pressed against the small of her back. She tried to go on tiptoes to rub her ass against him, but he tightened his arms.

"Stand still, Ellie."

She loved when he said her name. And she loved the feel of his hands making their way up her body. Her leotard was skintight, but the short sweater she wore over it provided a flimsy barrier that he skirted by pushing under it. She wasn't wearing a bra and her nipples peaked against his palms then ached when he pinched them between his thumbs and forefingers. The sound she made should've embarrassed her. Instead, Manny bent his head and bit her neck. As a reward, it was more effective than anything else he could've done. Well, almost anything else.

Because she knew how much better it could get. Was going to be.

"Take that off."

She knew he meant her sweater and tugged it over her head.

"Take your hair down."

She really should take issue with his bossy tone. Instead, she liked it. Not that she'd admit that, especially not to Manny, who would take that information and run with it. She'd seen this man at work.

Of course, right now, she didn't have a spine to speak of. Not with his hands running all over her body, squeezing her breasts and tweaking her nipples until she gasped with pleasure. Her hands were locked behind his downbent head, his lips pressing kisses along her neck.

He held her so tightly, she couldn't turn, and when she tried, his hands clamped on to her hips to hold her still.

"Do you want me, Ellie?"

His voice, spoken directly into her ear, made her shake with lust. "Yes."

"Even if I just want to lay you over the back of the couch and take you hard and fast?"

Oh god, yes.

She had to swallow down the knot in her throat before she could speak.

"Yes."

His hands tightened on her hips for several brief seconds before he pressed another blistering kiss against her nape. Then he walked her forward until they stood behind the couch.

"I'm going to strip you naked first. Get the condom out of my pocket."

She followed his orders—and they were orders—without thought because she wanted him to take her hard and fast. She was totally on board with his demanding hands pulling down her leotard, catching her tights on the way down. She'd toed off her sneakers before sitting down for dinner so her clothes slid off her body without hindrance, leaving her completely naked. A common occurrence around this man.

She could get used to that. Hell, she could get addicted to it. Especially when his hands slid from her ankles to her thighs to her hips, a rough caress sparking heat through her body that settled between her thighs. Her sex clenched as he molded one breast in his palm and let the other press low on her stomach.

Her breath stuttered out of her lungs, and her hands clenched onto the tops of the soft cushions of the couch.

"Lean forward."

His voice held a rough edge that made her entire body tense with desire. Bending over, she felt no self-consciousness, only an intense need to feel him inside her again. Her breasts flattened against the cushion, her arms reaching out to either side to hold herself steady.

"Don't move, Ellie. I just need to..."

She heard him moving behind her, heard his zipper release and the sound of the condom package tearing open.

"Are you on the pill?"

"Yes."

"Tomorrow I'll give you my medical clearance. I'm clean, but I need you to know that. Next time, I don't want anything between us."

God, she wanted that too. Now. But she appreciated that he wanted her to be sure about him.

"Okay." She took a deep breath. "Now, Manny."

She barely got the words out before he stroked his hand between her legs, his fingers playing along her folds.

"Christ, you're wet."

She was. And aching. She wanted to be filled, wanted him to make her scream. And she wanted Rob to be there to watch and to hold her while he did. To take her—

She shook her head, her hair falling around her face like a shield.

Not fair. Not fair to Manny.

All rational thought stopped when his cock slid between her thighs, the tip rubbing against her clit before sinking inside. She moaned as she stretched around him, her body opening to accept him, pull him in, and tighten around him.

And when he began to move, she let her body drift into that

space between rational and fantasy. The physical act kept her grounded, the motion of his cock shuttling in and out of her body. But her mind let the fantasy grow, the fantasy where this meant more than just the act to him.

He gripped her hips with a fierce hold, heat rolling off his body. Though she was naked, she wasn't cold. Couldn't be cold. He set her on fire. The fact that she couldn't touch him just added fuel to the flame. Her fingers made dents in the cushions as his thrusts nailed her against the back of the couch.

She'd never had sex like this, hard and fast and on the edge. Never imagined she'd love it as much as she did. It made her want him to go harder, faster. Take her over the edge and let her fall.

But damn him, he began to slow.

"No. Manny. Don't."

"Don't what, hon?"

"Don't—"

His right hand slipped around her hip and unerringly found her clit.

Oh my god, his fingers were magic. They pinched and rubbed as he slowed his thrusts to what could only be considered glacial. She felt every inch of him scrape along her delicate inner tissue. She panted, hanging on the edge of an orgasm that he controlled. She tried to grind back against him but the hand on her hip clamped down, holding her in place.

"Manny." His name was a plea.

He thrust in deep, taking his own damn time.

"Hang on, Ellie. It'll be worth it."

Yes, she knew he'd deliver on his promise, but damn it, she was ready to scream. Which was what he wanted. He wanted to control her. And damn it, she let him. Gave herself over to him and felt the second he realized she'd done it.

He groaned, low and deep in his chest, as his fingers worked her harder, faster, and his cock seemed to swell inside her. Then he rocked into her, his hips snapping forward in a now-uneven rhythm, until finally, the tension inside her snapped and she did cry out as she came, her pussy clenching around his cock.

She didn't even realize that his arms had come around her body to hold her up as he pumped his own release into her body.

MANNY WANTED to close his eyes as he came inside Ellie's tight pussy, but he didn't want to accidentally hurt her by losing complete control. They were so tightly entwined and so close to the couch, he didn't want to move the wrong way and risk any harm.

So he forced himself to keep his eyes open and loosen his hold on her. Even though he didn't want to. He pulled out of her much sooner than he wanted, consoling himself with the thought that he'd be inside her again soon. Like in minutes, if he had his way. First, though, he had to get her in a bed. He'd been too damn impatient to take her upstairs before, but now he needed to do that.

And maybe then he'd text Rob and tell him to get his ass over here when he got back from Maryland so he could feel this fucking amazing too. He had a feeling Rob needed Ellie just as much as Manny did.

"Come on, sweetheart. Let's find a bed."

Swinging her into his arms, he looked down, but Ellie had already tucked her head under his chin and rested her cheek on his shoulder, her arms wrapped around his neck. He liked the weight of her in his arms, liked the way she felt, warm and soft, against his chest. He'd thought about her all day, hadn't been able to concentrate on work for longer than a few minutes before flashes of Sunday night intruded. And he'd known then.

She was theirs. He knew it in his gut.

Rob had been right about one thing. Manny had skeletons in his closet. But he'd salted and burned those bones long ago. He knew exactly why he and Ellie needed Rob for this relationship to work. Because without him, Manny wouldn't be enough.

He knew his strengths and weaknesses, knew what he could offer her and what he couldn't. Together, he and Rob would be able to give her what she needed.

Walking up the open staircase to his bedroom, he pulled the covers down and laid her close to the center of his bed. It was a king, because he liked to have room when he slept, but he knew he wouldn't mind having Ellie crowded against him all night long.

Rolling onto her back, she looked up at him, a slight smile on her beautiful mouth, her hand reaching out to the edge of the bed where he stood.

"Are you just going to stand there?"

"No, but I need to check my phone."

She continued to hold his gaze. "Rob."

He nodded, pulling the sheet over her body so she didn't get cold. And so he wasn't tempted to strip and crawl into bed with her and not bother to call Rob.

"He had a family thing today. And he wasn't thrilled about it."

"He and his dad don't get along, do they?"

"That's an understatement."

She paused for a moment. "He's lucky to have you."

"Why do you say that?"

"As a friend. Everyone needs someone who looks out for them."

He thought about it for a second then nodded. "We've looked out for each other for a long time."

"You have a good relationship."

They did. He wanted to make it stronger by including Ellie. A few months ago, he would've said that was crazy. That it wouldn't work. Today, he knew that it would.

Ellie began worrying her bottom lip with her teeth, her gaze darting away. He reached out to run his fingers along her jaw.

"Why does that bother you?"

"I don't want to be the cause of problems between you and Rob."

"Why do you think you would be?"

Her lips pursed as she rolled into a seated position, wrapping the sheet around her body and depriving him of the sight of her naked breasts. Probably for the best.

"This situation is problematic."

His arms crossed over his chest as his back straightened. "How so?"

Huffing, she waved between them. "If it was just us, sure, it most likely wouldn't be an issue. But Rob was with us Sunday night. I had sex with you *and* I had sex with Rob. But tonight it was just you. Don't you think that's going to cause problems between the two of you? Unless..."

When she didn't continue, he tapped her chin with his index finger.

"Unless what?" he prompted.

She took a deep breath and released it before answering, her gaze snapping back to his.

"Unless nothing." She shook her head. "Go. Check on Rob. Tell him...I hope everything went okay."

He debated his next words for all of two seconds. "Tell him yourself. We can call him."

"But then he'll know..."

Another pause. "Know what?"

She rolled her eyes. "That we're together. Without him." Another huff. "You know what? This conversation isn't going anywhere so let's just forget it. Call Rob. I need to get dressed."

"No, you don't. Why do you need to get dressed if you're staying?"

Her gaze narrowed. "Who said I was staying?"

He bit back a smile. "Why are you leaving?"

"Because I have my own home."

"Stay here tonight."

The look on her face told him everything he needed to know. The immediate excitement that flashed through her eyes.

"Why?"

"Because I want you to. I want you here. I want to know you're in bed with me. If Rob's home, I'll tell him to come over. You want him here too, don't you?"

"I..." She blinked at him, clearly flustered.

"It's okay to say yes, Ellie."

"Do you want me to say yes?"

He shook his head. "It's gotta be what you want."

"And if I don't know what I want? How can I know what I want when I have no idea what this even is?"

"What 'what' is?"

"Us. This." She scowled up at him. "Why are you being so damn difficult?"

Bending down, he planted his fists into the mattress on either side of her thighs, their eyes on the same level. "Because I want you to realize that I don't just want an affair, or a couple nights of sex and then we're done. I want more. For the three of us."

She looked stunned, but he understood. She'd get over it. Because he was fairly certain she wanted the same.

"I don't know what I'm supposed to say to that." She shook her head, but she didn't look like she wanted to say no.

"Say you understand and are on board."

"We spent one night together."

"We've known each other for years." He wasn't backing down on this. Not now. "I've wanted you for *years*. So has Rob. We just didn't know how to make a relationship like this work. Until now."

It kinda pissed him off that he hadn't considered a three-some before, that it had taken Ryan and Chase's relationship for him to see the light. But now that he had, he was going to make it his fucking life's mission to make it work.

Her eyes had gotten wider with his every word. "Years?"

"Are you seriously telling me you had no idea?"

She nodded. "Why did you never ask me out?"

"Because I knew Rob had the same feelings and we were employed by your dad's company. Those were some pretty heavy barriers to overcome."

"But you're over them now?"

She sounded hopeful, her eyes brighter, her lips edging toward a smile. It made him smile in return and her entire demeanor shifted. Her eyes brightened and a grin broke free. And damn, if that didn't hit him like a punch in the gut. It should've been a warning. Your dreams didn't come true after one night and the best sex of your life.

But with Ellie in his bed grinning at him, Manny wanted his fucking happily-ever-after. He wanted Ellie. He wanted Rob to stop obsessing over his life and his family and settle the fuck down. He wanted the three of them to create the family he'd never had. A family he wanted and would fight for until he got what he wanted, or it blew up in his face in the worst way and he buried himself in a hole and never looked back.

"Yeah. I'm over them. But I have to warn you. You say yes and you have me. But that means you're ours."

Her head tilted to the side and her hand rose to cup his cheek, her fingers lightly trailing over his lips, making him bite back the urge to crush her into the bed and take her again.

"How could you not have known I've been lusting after you and Rob for years?"

"Maybe because I wasn't looking."

"But you see it now, right? That I want this?"

He grabbed her hand and nipped at her fingertips, drawing a smile from her. "You've got to be sure. You've seen what Whitney has had to deal with. The looks. The innuendo. The gossip. Even though people don't come right out and say it to her face, they're talking about her behind her back."

"The only people whose opinions matter to me are you, Rob, my friends, and Jack."

"That's a whole other issue we're going to need to address."

"I know."

Her expression made it clear she wasn't looking forward to that conversation, and he didn't blame her. He knew how much Jack meant to her and how much his opinion meant. Hell, it meant almost as much to Manny. Jack was more than just his boss. He was the one person Manny looked up to most, and he knew Jack was going to be blindsided by this relationship. And probably not happy about it.

"Jack wants me to be happy. You make me happy. Rob..." she grinned, "makes me want to strangle him. But..."

"You can be honest with me, Ellie. That's the only way this works."

She stared into his eyes for a long second. "I want him too. I loved what happened Sunday night. Does that make me—"

He leaned and kissed the rest of the words off her lips.

"It doesn't make you anything other than a desirable

woman. Trust me, Ellie. He wants you. I want you. Rob just may need some convincing that we can make this work."

Her fingers froze. "Can we?"

He heard hesitation in her voice and the desire to be reassured. He wanted to give her anything she wanted. "Yes. We can."

He'd back those words up with sheer determination.

"ROB. HANG ON A MINUTE."

Damn it. He'd been about to make a clean getaway. The photographer was still inside putting her equipment away, he'd said good-bye to his mom and had told his sister and Nan that he'd see them tomorrow. The last he'd seen his dad, he'd been talking to the journalist. Rob had figured he was safe to make his escape.

Halting by his car, parked in the circular driveway of his parents' Maryland home, he turned to face his dad, schooling his expression into a blank mask. "I need to get on the road. Early morning meeting."

Not necessarily a lie. There were always meetings. Just because he didn't have one specifically tomorrow morning didn't mean there wouldn't be one.

"You're busy. I understand. Your mom appreciates you taking the time out of your busy schedule for your family."

Rob's teeth ground at his dad's patronizing tone. "Whatever Mom needs."

No fighting. No fighting. No fighting.

The photographer and journalist were still here. His mom didn't need the tabloids getting wind of stress between him and his dad. So Rob would play nice until he got the hell out of here.

"She's grateful for your support."

Great talk, Dad.

Time to go. He had the door to his car open and was ready to get in, when his dad said, "She won't ask you, because she believes she knows what your answer will be. But I will. She wants you to run her campaign."

That made his head swing around. "What?"

"She believes you can help her win."

Rob's brain skipped like a rock over still water. "She wants me to be her campaign manager?"

His dad nodded, the faint smile on his lips not at all what his fans would expect from him. But here, there were no cameras. He didn't have to be "on" for anyone.

"She does. She's been looking for someone for months, but none have been the right fit. She doesn't want a 'political hack mired in archaic traditions.' Your mom's words, not mine." Another half smile. "She thinks you'd bring a fresh perspective to the campaign."

Surprise held him silent while his brain processed his dad's words. And then began to run with them. Was this the challenge he'd been looking for? Philly was only a couple of hours from his mom's campaign headquarters in Bel Air. He could stay close to Manny and Ellie without feeling like a constant third wheel.

"You don't need to give her an answer tonight. A move like this requires thought."

Yeah, it would. Because he didn't want to say yes for the wrong reasons.

"Your sister's worried about you. You know that, right? And frankly, so are your mom and I."

Rob shook his head, his brain trying to follow the shift in his dad's conversation.

"I don't know why. There's nothing to be worried about."

"You and me, we're a lot alike." His dad held up a hand

before Rob's automatic denial left his lips. "I know you don't want to hear it, but it's true. We don't trust easily, and we have trouble expressing our emotions. Better to not have attachments than to have them ripped away from you."

That one hit a little too close to home for comfort. "I have friends."

"And from what I understand, they're good friends. Fairhaven was good for you. Another of your mom's decisions. I didn't want to send you away. I thought we could figure it out on our own. Your mom's much smarter than I will ever be."

Rob couldn't argue with that last statement. His mom was one of the smartest people he knew. And she loved his dad. Those two facts had never made sense.

"I'm fine, Dad. Everything's going well at work."

Liar. You haven't been happy at work for months.

"So you're still happy playing with other people's money and throwing yourself off mountains?"

Rob swore he heard his jaw crack.

Don't respond. Just get in the car and drive a way.

"I know you don't believe what I do has any merit—"

"That's not true. Not at all. I just think it's not right for you. I think it's why you've been so unsettled lately. Why you jump off those mountains. And why your mom and sister are worried about you."

"But not you."

Another smile, this one fleeting. "Of course I worry. I've just learned that no matter what I say, it's not going to matter. And no matter what I say, you'll do the exact opposite. So I've learned to keep my mouth shut." A huff of amusement. "Trust me, it's been tough."

"You want me to believe your dissatisfaction with my life is *my* fault?"

Another laugh from his dad, this one louder and longer.

"Don't take this the wrong way, kid, but you sound just like me about forty years ago with my dad. I don't know what your granddad hated more. That I refused to go to college and learn a respectable trade or that I was good at the whole acting thing."

Rob's brain stuttered over that, because he remembered his granddad bragging about his son, the famous actor, to anyone who'd listen at the retirement home where he spent the last years of his life.

"Look, kid, I'm really not trying to tell you how to live your life. But your mom and your sister are worried about you. Do you honestly think Sarafina wants to move to Philadelphia?"

"Safi's been talking about moving away from LA for years. She always said she didn't want to raise children there."

"But Philly?" His dad's eyebrows rose about a centimeter of an inch, just enough to make Rob's blood heat. "There's only one reason why your sister moved to Philly."

The worst part was, his dad was right and Rob knew it. No matter how much he'd tried, his parents and sister had never allowed him to drift too far away for too long.

Maybe that's why you've always known there'd be someone at the other end of the chain, tugging you back to the ground.

The problem had always been, he didn't want to be tied down.

"We see you becoming unmoored and we're worried. All of us. I also know you don't want to hear it, especially from me. So talk to Manny. I know you'll listen to him. We don't want to lose you again."

NINE

Wednesday morning, Manny paused outside Rob's office and nearly rapped his knuckles on the closed door.

It felt strange. He'd never knocked before. But for the first time in a long time, he felt a distance between him and Rob. He fucking hated it.

Fuck it. He grabbed the lever and pushed through.

"Hey. How'd it go yesterday?"

Rob turned his chair away from the window and stared at Manny for a few seconds before shaking his head. "It was...interesting."

"You want to talk about it?"

He expected Rob to say no, so he was surprised when Rob waved at the door. "Shut that first."

Surprise quickly turned into a sense of foreboding that sat in his gut like a lead ball. With the door closed, Manny sank into the seat opposite Rob and waited for the other shoe to drop.

"What was so interesting?"

"Mom wants me to manage her campaign."

Well, shit.

Carefully choosing his words, Manny said, "Is she serious?"

Rob nodded. "She said she wants someone she can trust at her side, helping her make decisions from the start."

"Makes sense." And it did. A little too much for Manny's comfort. "Is this something you want to do?"

Rob sighed hard, his gaze darting to the window again. "I don't know. It's not something I ever considered."

"And now that you have?"

Rob paused before meeting Manny's gaze again. "I'm considering it."

Yeah, that's what Manny figured.

"When does she need you?"

"Immediately."

Of course. Taking his time, Manny sat in the chair opposite Rob's desk, forcing himself not to cross his arms over his chest. "Sounds like you've made up your mind."

Rob shook his head. "Dad said I should talk to you first."

Okay, that was a surprise. "Why me?"

"Because he knows I trust you."

Fuck. That felt like a low blow. Even if it was true. Rob trusted Manny to tell him the truth. So he would.

"I think if you want to do it, you should. You're not happy here. You haven't been for a while. It'd be a new challenge. Something to sink your teeth into."

Rob didn't look surprised. But he didn't exactly look happy either.

"Come with me." Rob leaned forward onto his desk, his expression intently serious. "She's going to need security. We can continue to work together. We've talked about going out on our own before. This could be a new start."

Surprise, and a niggle of something that felt like curiosity bloomed deep in Manny's gut before he shut it down. He couldn't leave. Not now.

Could I?

"What about Ellie?"

Rob's gaze didn't flicker. "If you want to continue seeing her, Bel Air is only a couple hours away from Philly."

Manny noticed how careful Rob had been with his words. "And if I don't want to leave Perrault?"

"No harm, no foul." Rob shook his head. "Our friendship doesn't change."

But it would. Manny knew Rob wanted him to come with him. And he had to admit it sounded interesting. A new challenge to conquer. But it would force him to leave Ellie. And he didn't want to give her up.

"Rob—"

"Think about it, Manny. That's all I'm saying."

"You want me to choose."

"No, I don't." Rob's expression didn't change at all. "But I can't stay. I'm drowning. I need to get out."

Manny knew that. He'd known Rob needed to do something else with his life. He just hadn't been able to say the words. But he didn't want to give up Ellie. He didn't want to give up the promise of the relationship the three of them could create.

"And what are you going to do about Ellie?" Manny intentionally repeated his earlier question, knowing Rob had avoided answering the first time.

Rob's pause gave Manny the answer Rob didn't want to speak.

"You owe her an explanation."

Rob's gaze blinked away for a second. "I planned to ask her over for dinner tonight. I'll tell her then."

Manny noticed Rob hadn't include him. And Manny didn't have a problem with that. He couldn't. Jealousy of any kind had no place in this kind of relationship. It couldn't, not if they wanted this to work. Although Rob seemed determined to blow it to hell.

"Tell her what?"

"That I'm leaving."

"You made up your mind in the past five minutes?"

"My dad was right." Rob grimaced. "I needed to talk to you. You help me see things more clearly. I think this change would be good for both of us. And it clears the way for you and Ellie to date without looking like you're fucking your way to the top."

"GOOD AFTERNOON, Miss Perrault. How are you today?"

Ellie's head snapped up at the sound of Rob's voice. She'd been reading letters from various charities around the country, asking for money. It was one of the jobs she both loved and hated, because she could help others, but there were always more demands for money than actual budgeted funds, which sucked.

She didn't respond to Rob immediately, because there were so many things running through her head. Not the least of which was memories of Sunday night. It was Wednesday afternoon. That made her angry. Not that she had anything to be angry about. It wasn't like they were dating.

They'd had sex. Once. That was all. Really good sex, but still.

"Hello, Mr. Henry. What can I do for you?"

She tried not to let that anger seep into her voice. Apparently, she didn't do a very good job because his mouth twisted in a wry grin that still managed to be sexy as hell. Damn him.

"I was hoping you'd agree to go out to dinner with me tonight."

"Oh." She blinked, lips parted as her brain tried to make connections. That was the last thing she'd expected to hear from him. And the one thing she wanted. And shouldn't. "I guess...that'd be okay. Will—" She shook her head. "Never mind."

His brows arched. "Will Manny be there? Do you want him to come?"

Did she? "Not if you don't want him there."

Rob's expression was unexpectedly serious. "If it's okay with you, I'd like to talk to you alone."

This was sounding more and more like a conversation she didn't want to have. Like a breakup. Considering they'd gone on exactly one date and had wild sex in a tub, he probably could've just texted her to tell her, "Hey, thanks for the other night. See you around the office sometime."

And she would've made sure she never saw him in the office again.

"Okay, sure."

"Are you ready to leave?"

She blinked up at him. "Now?"

His smile set her heart racing. "It's almost six-thirty. What are you doing here so late, anyway?"

She glanced at the time on her monitor screen. It read 6:26.

"I had no idea what time it was. I've been going through wish requests. I like to do a lot of them at one time." Saved on her mascara usage. They always made her cry.

"If you don't want to go out, we can order food in. Your place or mine?"

Alone with him? She really shouldn't. But if he was going to tell her the other night was a mistake, and they weren't going to be seeing each other again... Did she really want to have the conversation in a restaurant?

"Your place? Bailey's home tonight." And she really didn't want to be dumped with an audience.

"Sure. Do you need a few more minutes or are you ready to leave now?"

Pasting on a smile, she shut down her computer, grabbed her purse, and stood, heading for the door. He didn't move out of her way so she could walk through. Instead, she found her footsteps faltering as she got closer to the door.

Damn him, he was just so good-looking. She didn't consider herself a shallow person, but she couldn't take her eyes off him. Which was so confusing because she still wasn't sure she even liked him.

Liar. You like him a little too much.

And he was going to break her heart.

Little overdramatic, don't you think?

She was afraid it wasn't.

"Is something wrong?" she asked, when he made it clear he wasn't moving right away.

He lifted a hand to stroke it down her cheek, a totally unexpected action that made her react with an audible intake of air. Bright blue eyes narrowed down to slits, he let his gaze slip down to her mouth. Which made her swallow hard, her lips parting.

Would he kiss her? She really wanted him to kiss her.

Several seconds passed while she waited for him to make a move. But when he did, it wasn't the one she wanted. He straightened away from the doorjamb, his head now inches above hers, and waved her through the door.

Twenty minutes later, they arrived at his condo, after a short car ride that'd been quietly subdued. His home was exactly what she'd expected. Sleek, contemporary furniture, lots of gray walls and an open-concept plan. The place had no life. Not at all like Manny's home.

"How long have you lived here?"

Closing the door behind her, he shed his suit jacket and waved a hand toward the couch in the living area.

"A few years. Make yourself comfortable. I'll be right out."

He disappeared through a doorway in the back. She was tempted to follow, to watch him strip off his clothes. But that would be a total invasion of his privacy. Wouldn't it?

With a sigh, she walked over to the couch he'd indicated. It didn't look comfortable at all. She had to wonder if anyone ever sat on it.

The two chairs in front of the wide windows looking out over the city looked much more inviting. Toeing off her sandals, she settled on the chair on the right, sinking into the plush cushions with a little sigh. Tucking her legs beneath her, she settled the skirt of her casual sundress around her legs, thankful for the cropped sweater she'd worn over her dress. Rob kept his home as cold as a refrigerator, though it probably only seemed that way since it was close to ninety degrees outside again today. The east coast was in the grip of a heat wave, and she'd dressed for it.

"I turned down the air conditioning. Should warm up in a few seconds. Sorry about that."

"No...problem."

Well, damn. He'd changed into jeans and a t-shirt. Simple enough, but the jeans fit him like a second skin and the t-shirt matched his eyes and clung to his well-defined chest. She bit her bottom lip so she wouldn't make any stupid sounds. Like sighing.

"Food should be here soon." He walked toward the kitchen and now she checked out his mighty nice ass. "Want something to drink? Wine, lemonade, or beer?"

"Lemonade, thank you." Probably better not to tempt fate with alcohol.

A few seconds later he handed her a glass then sat in the chair next to hers. He'd gone for lemonade too.

"Nice view."

"I think so." But he wasn't staring out the window. He was staring at her.

Heat began to pop through her body. She tried to tamp it down. "Was there a reason you wanted to have dinner?"

"I want to talk to you."

"What do you want to talk about?"

He didn't say anything right away, his gaze holding hers. She didn't have a clue what he was thinking. And then he smiled, though it didn't seem to reach his eyes.

"I'm sorry I missed dinner with you and Manny last night. My mom is running for Maryland Senate. She had a photo shoot and interview yesterday to announce her run."

"I heard. You must be really proud."

"My mom's brilliant. She cares about people, but she doesn't take any bullshit. She'll make a great politician because she's focused."

Ellie laughed. "She sounds amazing."

"She is." He paused. "She wants me to run her campaign."

She didn't connect the dots right away. It took her a few seconds to understand what he was saying. And when she did, she felt that heat drain away in a split second.

"You're leaving Perrault."

"I haven't told Jack yet, but yeah. My mom needs me to start as soon as possible. I wanted to tell you before you heard from anyone else."

She wasn't sure what to say. It felt like a little piece of her heart had been nicked away. Which was stupid. They'd spent one night together.

"I guess...congratulations are in order."

A bell rang and Rob grimaced, as if he were about to say something.

"Hold that thought. Food's here."

She had a few seconds to collect herself while he went to

the door. So this was good-bye. He was leaving. She felt like someone had reached inside her chest and squeezed her lungs. She tried to breathe normally but had to suck in air quickly when she realized he was on his way back. Forcing a smile, she followed him to the dining table, where he was setting the bags.

"I think I'll take that beer now."

He snapped a quick look at her as he paused while pulling out the food.

"Sure. Do you wanna..."

"I'll get the food out."

By the time he got back, she had the food on the table and had taken a seat. Rob sat across from her after he set the beer by her plate. Silence held for a few seconds while they dished out Buddha's Delight and General Tso's chicken. Rob kept the discussion focused on his mom's senate run and what his role would be in her campaign. He managed to keep any awkward silences at bay.

They were cleaning up the dishes when he said, "I need a change. I feel like I've been stagnating recently."

She thought of what she should say and settled on, "The company will miss you."

He didn't respond immediately, his gaze searching hers until she wanted to look away. But wouldn't. "Will *you* miss me?"

She forced herself to maintain his gazes. "Do you want me to miss you?"

A tiny muscle in his jaw twitched, the only outward sign she was affecting him.

"I can't stay," he finally said. "I wouldn't be doing anyone any favors if I did."

"I don't need any favors."

Frustration made his brow furrow. "That's not what I meant. I need to do this for myself."

"And I hope it works out for you."

He leaned back in his chair, his gaze laser-focused on her. "Do you?

"Of course. I mean," she shrugged, "you have sex with me one night and tell me you're leaving the next. Might give another girl a complex."

He paused for a second. "But not you."

"You made it clear the other night you weren't interested in anything other than sex."

His gaze narrowed even farther. "I don't believe I said that."

She reached for her beer, forcing herself to hold Rob's gaze. "I'm good at reading between the lines."

"But you're not reading this situation right. My leaving has nothing to do with you."

She shrugged again and she swore she saw his jaw clench. "I guess that's good to know."

"Do you need me to prove it?"

Her head tilted to the side, her gaze a challenge. "Do you feel the need to prove it?"

* * *

ROB SPRAWLED BACK in his chair, his expression firming into hard lines.

He felt like an asshole. Yep. That was him. The asshole. But he was trying to find a graceful way out of this situation for all of them. He didn't, for one minute, believe she wanted a long-lasting poly relationship. They'd had fun. And if she wanted to have one last go at him before he left, he wasn't opposed.

Hell, he was all for it. Even though there was a little voice in the back of his brain that kept telling him they were missing someone. Which was bullshit. They didn't need Manny. They could have sex just fine without him.

Wouldn't be as good.

He wanted to tell himself to shut the fuck up. Right here, right now, this was between him and Ellie.

"Do you want me to tell you to come over here and straddle my lap so I can prove to you that my leaving Perrault doesn't mean I don't want to fuck you again?"

He wondered if he'd pushed too far when she didn't say anything right away. She didn't look upset as she took another sip of her beer. Her lips wrapped around the mouth of the bottle made his cock twitch. And when she drew the bottle away from her mouth, he followed her tongue as it slipped out to lick her lip and catch the drop of beer that lingered there.

Holy fuck. How did she do this to him? How did she make him crave her and want to run in the opposite direction at the same time?

A second later, she leaned forward and set the beer on the table to her right. Then she stood.

"I've always been a sucker for a challenge," she said. "You probably don't know that about me. You have this image in your head of the girl you think I am. But that's not me."

Before he knew what she intended, she stripped off her little sweater and walked toward him. Her dress had a flowy skirt that brushed her knees and a collared top. What he hadn't known because she'd been wearing that little sweater was that it was a halter dress. Completely covered her from neck to knees in the front. But when she turned to drop the sweater on the chair she'd just left, he saw how it bared her entire back.

His fingers curled almost painfully into the chair arms. Definitely going to leave marks. Especially when she unhooked the clasp at her neck and the front of the dress fell to her waist.

Christ, she was beautiful. Sleek and rounded and his mouth watered just looking at her. His cock ached, needing her.

She stared down at him, daring him to...what? Grab her and

throw her on the floor? He wanted to, but it wasn't going to happen. He forced himself to remain in the chair because she didn't appear to be finished. His gaze locked on hers as her hands swept around her waist. Seconds later, the dress slid off her body to the floor.

Now she stood before him in only a pair of pure white lace panties that threatened to make him drool. He'd be lying if he didn't admit she took his breath away. His cock hardened, his balls drawn up tight. The greedy desire to fuck her consumed him, to pull her down onto his lap, sink inside her, and release this pent-up need that ate at his gut.

Instead, he forced himself to reach for her slowly. Leaning forward, he grabbed her by the hips and tugged her closer. She came without complaint, her breath hitching when he gripped the strings holding her panties together and pulled them off her hips. They were so delicate, he was afraid he'd tear them, so he took his time. Every muscle in his body wanted to rip them away.

Instead, he tortured himself, denying the need that ate at him, until he'd dragged the scrap of lace to her knees then let it fall to the floor. His gaze swept up her naked body, his heart pounding and his blood on fire. He had his hands on her hips in the next second and lifted her off her feet, settling her on her knees over his lap. Her fingers were already working on opening his pants when he cupped her face in his hands and kissed her.

The second his eyes closed and their lips meshed, he lost all sense of anything but her. He lost himself in her.

Her fingers worked the button at his waistband eagerly, quickly followed by the release of his zipper. His cock ached with the knowledge that she was about to wrap her fingers around him. Letting one hand curve around her nape, he moved the other down her body, cupping the curve of a breast before sliding down to her hip. Need rode him hard, urging him to tug her closer, his kiss becoming more demanding. She gave him what he wanted, exactly how he wanted. But he still wanted more.

The hand on her hip slid between her thighs, his fingers sliding along the folds of her sex. Moaning into his mouth at his touch, she gripped his shoulders hard, her fingers biting into his skin. The slight pain triggered a response deep inside, a rush of emotion so fierce, he could barely contain it. It felt like desperation.

Shoving that emotion to one side, he released her hip and shoved down his now-open jeans to free his cock. Her hands gripped his shoulders as she positioned her hips and began to sink onto his shaft. She'd almost taken all of him when he realized he wasn't wearing a condom.

Releasing her mouth, he grabbed her hips in both hands and held her steady, even though every muscle in his body was screaming for him to bury himself completely inside her.

She must have read his mind. "I'm on the pill." Her voice was barely a whisper, husky and rough. "Come inside me."

"I'd never harm you, Ellie."

She nodded. "I know. Now shut up and move."

Her mouth covered his as she wriggled her hips and blew his control to pieces. He yanked her down, her slick sheath encasing him in heat. The sound she made... He nearly came without moving a muscle.

He knew he wasn't going to last long, but he also couldn't slow down. And Ellie didn't seem to want to slow down, either. She rocked her hips, her rhythm frantic and her kisses almost desperate. Her urgency infected him, his heart racing to keep up as he thrust harder, faster.

Until he had to slow down or lose his control.

Locking one arm around her waist, he held her in place, her body trembling above his. He let his cock swell inside her for as long as he could take it. His lungs burned but he refused to release her mouth. Every second felt like an eternity, as he tried to hold back the inevitable. Until he couldn't.

He had to move again. Releasing her mouth, he sucked in air as he opened his eyes, waiting for her to do the same. When she did, he loosened his hold.

"Slow, Ellie. Make me beg for it."

Her eyes dark with desire, she rubbed her nose against his.

"I thought you were."

Her fingers threaded through his hair, tugging until his scalp burned, adding to the sensations keeping his body on the edge of meltdown.

"Move, sweetheart. Get yourself off first. I wanna feel you come around my cock."

Her eyes fluttered shut for a second and her throat moved as she swallowed hard. And her sex tightened like a fist around him. He groaned, a deep sound almost like a growl. Now, she smiled, a sexy tilt of her lips that fucking slayed him.

Leaning closer, she spoke against his lips. "Say 'please.'"

Fuck, he was going to come if she said another goddamn word.

"Please. Fuck me, Ellie."

She rocked her hips, slow this time, her body moving in a sinuous dance on his cock. He broke out in a sweat, his hands curved around her ribs. His thumbs brushed against the underside of her breasts before he moved to fill his palms with them. He squeezed her tight, almost to the point of being too much. Except she arched into his hands, wanting more.

Bouncing on his lap, she worked toward an orgasm they both could just about touch. He was holding back but she was reaching, reaching...until finally, she moaned and her back arched. Her head fell onto his shoulder as she sank down, her sex convulsing around him.

She tried to take him with her, but he managed to hold off his own orgasm with sheer determination. Waiting.

And when she finally collapsed against him, limp, he lifted her without dislodging his cock, laid her out on the cushions of the nearest couch and rocked into her hard and fast until he came so hard, he swore he saw stars.

———

ROB WATCHED Ellie emerge from the powder room, dressed and looking as unruffled as the moment she'd walked through the door. And realized this was good-bye.

Tomorrow, he'd talk to Jack and negotiate his exit. He didn't think Jack would give him much of a hassle. It'd be a shock. Then again, maybe not. Maybe Jack would be happy to see him go. He wouldn't have to worry about Rob jumping off mountains anymore. Wouldn't have unhappy rich people breathing down his neck.

Rising from the couch, where he'd pulled on his pants and shirt, he waited for her to stop in front of him, his gut in a knot. But he couldn't go back on his word to his mom, which he'd given this morning. She'd been ecstatic. He knew he'd made the right decision because he was anxious as hell to get started. A new challenge. A new adventure.

But first...an ending.

When Ellie reached him, he couldn't tell what she was thinking. She'd never been good at hiding her emotions. She was doing a damn fine job right now.

"Will I see you at the office tomorrow?" Her voice didn't waver at all. "Do you plan to talk to Jack?"

"I do."

"Then I guess I won't see you. I'm sure you'll have a lot of stuff to figure out before you leave. When will that be, exactly?"

"As soon as Jack releases me from my contract. If he holds me to it, I'll be there at least a month. If not—"

"I can talk to Jack, get him to release you early. If that's what you want."

Yeah, it was. But she didn't have to sound so damn anxious to get rid of him.

"If you think it'll help, then yeah, I'd appreciate it."

She shrugged, just a quick lift of her left shoulder. "Of course. It's my company, after all." She paused, her gaze darting away for a brief second before meeting his again. "I hope you find what you're looking. Stay safe."

Before he could respond, she turned, picked up her purse, and walked out the door.

The knock on Ellie's office door Thursday afternoon was expected. She'd gotten a text from Rob that morning, telling her he was on his way to talk to Jack. Guess it was time to fulfill her promise.

"Jack. Hi." She conjured up a smile for her godfather, when honestly, she'd rather not have to deal with this now. Hell, she didn't know when she'd ever want to deal with this. "What are you doing down here?"

Jack's expression was strangely somber as he walked through the door. "I know you're not involved in the day-to-day operation of the company, but as the owner and principal stockholder, I thought you should know—"

"Rob's leaving. Yes, I've heard."

Jack paused, his gaze narrowed down to slits. Finally, he sighed, shaking his head. "So the rumors are true."

Rumors? What rumors?

"You *were* dating," Jack continued. "Is that why he decided to leave? Did something happen? Did he do something—"

"No, Jack. Rob didn't do anything." She shook her head, her

mouth twisting in a rueful grimace. "And we weren't really dating. It was just...a fling."

Jack's gaze now glittered with anger. "A fling. Guess that explains why he said you'd back his immediate resignation. Well, then. The sooner he leaves, the better. Or I may need the advice of a lawyer after I smack him down for hurting you."

Rising, Ellie walked across the room to give her godfather a tight hug, getting one in return that nearly squeezed the breath out of her.

She hadn't really had time to process anything since last night. She'd gone home, gone straight to bed, and had overslept this morning. Luckily, her first meeting hadn't been until eleven a.m. And she'd nearly been late for that. It was almost five now. She'd be leaving soon, curling up in comfy clothes, and splitting a pizza with Bailey, if her roommate was even going to be home tonight. They hadn't seen a lot of each other lately.

She didn't know when she'd see Manny.

Taking a step back, she felt Jack release her reluctantly.

"Thanks, but I'm fine. Really. We weren't even truly dating." Just having amazing sex. "We were...exploring our options."

Jack didn't look convinced. "Do I even want to ask about the rumors of you dating Manny?" He grimaced, shaking his head. "I'm not asking, by the way. You'll get no judgment, sweetheart. I'm not a prude, and I'm not a saint. But if anyone hurts you, I will punch first and ask questions later."

I am not *going to cry.*

"I love you, Jack. I don't know if I say that enough. I don't know what I would've done without you after Daddy died."

"Love you too, sweetheart." He sighed, patting her on the back gently, as if he were afraid he'd hurt her. Then he sighed. "I really hate to lose the damn guy. He's amazing at what he does. But this move has been a long time coming. He hasn't been happy here for months."

She bit her lip to stave off tears. "I know. I hope he finds what he needs."

Jack didn't respond immediately, as if he could read so much more from her expression than she wanted him to.

"If he isn't smart enough to realize he should hold tight to you, he's not the right guy. And if Manny doesn't realize you're the best thing that could happen to him, well, then I need to hire smarter men."

Laughing despite feeling lost, Ellie shook her head.

"Please, no. I don't think I could take it."

MANNY STOOD in the door of Rob's office, watching Rob fill a box with...who knows what. Rob had never been the kind of guy to have personal shit sitting around.

"What exactly are you putting in that box? Didn't peg you for stealing office supplies."

Rob turned with a grin that didn't exactly reach his eyes.

"I've accumulated more shit than I thought."

And isn't that a loaded statement.

Rob paused, as if he'd had the same thought. Probably had. They'd known each other for a long time.

"You know," Rob spoke as if he were choosing his words carefully, "you can still come with me. Mom wants you to handle her security. She trusts you. And so do I."

Manny felt the stress that'd been eating at his gut intensify. "I'm not in the market for a new job."

Rob set the box aside and leaned back on his desk, his gaze intense. "Just think about it. There's no reason you can't continue to see Ellie and—"

"You're asking me to choose."

Rob's jaw clenched. "No, I'm not. But I am asking if this is all you want to do with your life."

Manny heard the edge creeping into Rob's voice, felt his own spine straighten with stubbornness. And something that felt a little like grief.

"I like what I'm doing."

"But it's just a job." Rob's hands tightened on the edge of the desk, the knuckles going white. "And it's holding you in place. Don't you want a new challenge?"

Yeah, he did. But not now, when he had so much to lose.

You're going to lose her anyway.

"I'm not going to desert Ellie. Not now."

"So talk to her. Tell her you need to make a change. If she wants you, she'll roll with it. You and I have been partners for a long time." Rob said those words like Manny didn't know that. "You of all people know I need a new challenge. I never wanted to be stuck in one place for too long. That's not who I am."

"Having roots doesn't mean you're stuck."

"Maybe I just don't want to be here anymore."

Manny tried not to take that personally. And Rob sighed, as if he'd realized too late what he'd said.

"Shit." He dropped his head, breaking the connection between them. "You know that's not what I meant. Goddammit, just think about it. We can still work together. And you can still have Ellie."

"Don't you mean we?"

Rob shook his head, his face losing all expression. "I'd never be more than a third wheel."

Manny felt the anger he'd been shoving down start to bubble up. "That's bullshit and you know it. Did last night feel like you were a third wheel?"

Rob blinked. "How'd you know—"

"Because I texted her and she told me she was having dinner with you."

Manny saw a chink in Rob's armor as a muscle in his jaw started to twitch. "I wanted to tell her I was leaving."

"You don't have to fucking explain yourself to me. But don't fucking lie. You wanted one last night with her. Except it doesn't have to be the last."

"Maybe I just don't want to work that hard at a relationship."

Manny's anger rose up like a wave now, threatening to drown him. "Maybe you're just too fucking scared to try."

Rob stilled, though his labored breathing belied his outward calm. "And maybe you just don't know me as well as you think you do. If you did, you'd know I've been throttling myself for the past year, trying to make myself fit in a role I'm not suited for."

"You think I don't know that? Of course I do. But you're letting the bullshit about this job interfere with your feelings for Ellie. And you're lying to yourself if you think you're not."

Rob had reached the end of his patience. Manny saw it in the flat line of his mouth and the anger in his eyes. "Jesus, can't you see she's in love with you? She has been for years. You don't need me to keep her."

"I don't want to keep her like a goddamn pet. I want a relationship. I believe the three of us together could be amazing."

"You don't need me to make you and Ellie work. You're enough for her."

Goddamn Rob. He knew exactly which of Manny's buttons to push. But he wasn't going to take the bait. "Maybe we all need each other more than you think."

ELLIE HADN'T EXPECTED to see Manny Friday, so when he showed up at her door around eight that night, she had the urge to grab him and not let go.

She knew, because her secretary told her, that Rob had stopped by her office before leaving the building today. She hadn't been there, not by design but because she'd had a class to teach. If he'd wanted to see her, he could've asked where to find her.

Instead, he'd called and left her a voice message, promising he'd be in touch next week. She hadn't deleted the message yet, but she wasn't sure how she was going to respond. Or if she was going to respond.

"Hi." She smiled, happy to see him as she waved him through the door, even though she couldn't shake the feeling they were missing a crucial piece of their puzzle. The sooner she moved beyond that, the better.

"Hey. Sorry I didn't call. I was in the neighborhood." He shook his head, his mouth curved in a wry grin. "And yeah, I know how that sounds, but it's true."

Leading him over to the couches, she sank onto the cushions, hoping he'd take the hint and sit with her. "You don't need an excuse to see me, you know."

He did take the hint and then made her heart race when he reached over and pulled her onto his lap. She went willingly, tucking her head under his chin and her arms around his shoulders. It felt right to have his arms around her.

"I know that. But, Ellie, I gotta warn you."

Oh no, that didn't sound good. She took a deep breath and looked up, prepared to see the old Manny who had never given her the time of day. But the look on his face was anything but dismissive. And her heart began to race.

"I'm not planning to be that guy you see once in a while to scratch an itch." His focus on her was intense and she had to admit she liked it. "I want all of you. Not just bits and pieces. I thought if it was the three of us, I wouldn't have to give all of myself. That if Rob was here, I wouldn't have to go all in. But I realized that's not going to work. Because I want everything from you. And you deserve the same from me."

Now her heart moved to her throat, and she had to swallow hard to be able to speak. "Good. Because I want everything you've got to give. I don't want to settle for anything less than all of you. If that's too much, tell me now and—"

Manny wrapped his hand around her nape and yanked her up against his chest, bringing his head down to kiss her, allowing all the pent-up desire and frustration to pour out of him.

And when she opened her mouth and her arms to him, she gave him everything he'd ever wanted.

***

"DO you want to go with him?"

Manny looked down at Ellie, a frown forming as her words penetrated the fog of lust still permeating his brain. They'd barely made it to her bedroom before they'd stripped each other naked. Luckily, Bailey was out for the night.

Her head rested on his chest, her hand on his abs, the soft brush of her breath against his skin lulling him into relaxation. Except for the twinge in his chest and a sense of anxiety he couldn't shake.

"What?"

"Do you want to work for Rob's mom?"

Manny took a beat before he answered. "How did you know she asked?"

She shrugged, her bare skin moving against his in a sensuous slide. "I didn't. Just a lucky guess. So why didn't you go?"

"Maybe I'm not ready to leave Perrault."

"I don't want you to stay just because of me."

"Do you want me to go?"

She paused and his heart seized. "I've always thought of you and Rob as partners. A force of nature together. I don't want to be the cause of a rift between you."

"This doesn't have anything to do with you."

Pushing herself onto her elbows, she stared down at him. Her hair fell in messy waves around her shoulders, her lips puffy from his kisses, but her eyes were laser-focused.

"I know that's not true. I also need you to know that I trust you. I want you to be happy. Not feel trapped."

"Wait, Ellie—"

She put two fingers over his lips, cutting off whatever he was going to say. "Are you happy at Perrault?"

"I'm extremely happy here with you."

Her mouth flattened into a line. "You know that's not what I meant. Stop deflecting."

"Would it make our relationship easier on you if I weren't at Perrault?"

She blinked and he watched her replay his words in her head, figuring them out. "What? No. Stop twisting my words."

"I'm not. I'm just trying to figure out what you're trying to say. Do you want me to go work for Rob's mom? I understand sleeping with someone who works for you can be an issue."

"I can't say I haven't thought about that," her nose crinkled adorably, "but not because of any blowback on me." She shook her head. "People will look at you differently when they find out we're dating."

"But it wouldn't be an issue if I left."

She shook her head, frustration making her frown. "I want you to do what makes you happy."

"Do you want me to leave?"

"Will that make you happy?"

He thought about his words before he spoke because he had the sense that question held a ticking time bomb.

"You make me happy."

Her smile was brilliant for the few seconds she flashed it. "I think that might be the sweetest thing anyone's ever said to me."

"No one's ever accused me of being sweet."

Her laughter filled the room, and the pit in his stomach widened just a little more. That pit had been gnawing at his nerves for days. He'd managed to keep it tamped down.

This would work. They would make it work. He wouldn't allow any other outcome.

"Manny," warmth had replaced the amusement in her voice, "does your work at Perrault make you happy?"

No. It was a simple answer for a not-so-simple question.

Her mouth screwed into a sad little twist when he didn't answer. "I think you should take the job with Rob's mom."

His jaw flexed against the immediate desire to say no. Because there was a part of him that admitted the only reason he didn't want to leave was her. And that seemed juvenile. Or at the very least, admission of a weakness. He had to be strong, had to hold this together for the three of them. Because losing her and losing Rob was not an option.

ELLIE WATCHED Manny struggle to come up with a response and realized she needed to breathe or she was going to pass out.

Her brain was still scrambled from the amazing sex they'd had only minutes ago and she couldn't believe she was already thinking about doing it again. Except this time, she'd be on top and Manny would let her do whatever she wanted to him. Because he wanted her to be happy. She was happy. It was just tempered by the fact that there was a huge, Rob-size hole in the bed next to her.

And because she wanted Manny to be happy too, she knew she was doing the right thing, pushing him toward something he wanted to do. But how did she reassure him and herself at the same time? They'd just found each other. But without Rob, would they ever feel complete?

"Ellie."

"Yes?"

Manny looked torn. She didn't blame him. Her lungs felt heavy, as if they were encased in cement. Then she watched his expression clear.

"You could come with us." He spoke with absolute certainty.

Confusion made her brow crinkle. "What? No, I can't." Could she?

"Yes, you can." Manny's voice held that bossy tone she loved in bed. "Bel Air is only a couple of hours from Philly. It'd require some juggling but that's life. Make the jump with us."

Was he asking her to live with them? That's what it sounded like to her. And oh, she wanted to be right. Could she do it? Could she leave everything for the chance at happiness with them? Would Rob even want to try?

"What about my students? I'm not going to leave them."

And she loved teaching. It wasn't just a job for her.

Manny wore his problem-solving face now. "We can find somewhere in the middle. Sure, it'll be tough while his mom campaigns, but when she gets elected, we can move somewhere between DC and Philly. It'll work."

Hope was a four-letter word. She wanted to take what he was offering, wanted to reach out and grab on with both hands. But failure could blow up three lives, not just two. And there was the very real possibility that Rob wouldn't go for it. He'd left without a backward glance two days ago. It already felt like forever.

"Do you think we're rushing things?"

Cupping her face in his hands, he tugged her closer so he could kiss her, long and hard. He laid claim to her mouth. And her heart.

"I think we should've done this years ago. I'm not waiting anymore. Rob will get on board. We won't give him a choice."

ELEVEN

"You look miserable."

Rob cocked an eyebrow at his sister, who'd just waddled through the door of his office in his mom's headquarters in Bel Air. And no, he would never say "waddle" aloud to his sister. He wasn't stupid.

"And you look too damn happy for a Tuesday morning. What are you doing here so early?"

Safi glared at him. "I'm pregnant, not incapacitated. And you're deflecting." She eased into the padded chair across from his desk. "Talk to me. What's going on?"

He shook his head, spreading his hands out over his desk. "About a million and one things at the moment. I'm just settling in. What do you need?"

Her eyebrows rose. "Think you bit off more than you can chew?"

Grinning at her challenge, he leaned back in his chair, hands folded over his stomach. "Ask me that in a month. But you're not here just to bust my ass. What's up?"

"Actually, I am here just to check up on you. Dad's afraid to piss you off and Mom's got her own shit to worry about. So it's just you and me. Everything happened so fast. This job, your move...you ending things with Ellie."

He tried not to let his surprise show, but damn it, how'd she know? "Ellie and I didn't end things. There was nothing to end."

"Mmhmm." Safi's neutral expression made his back teeth grind against each other. "So you don't miss her?"

Every damn second. It was like a constant ache he couldn't soothe, which really sucked because he couldn't do a damn thing about it.

"There's nothing to miss." He wondered who he was trying to convince, Safi or himself. "We spent a couple of nights together. We didn't pledge our undying love. It wasn't a big deal."

She shrugged, like it meant nothing to her. "And Manny? Have you talked to him since you left?"

No. The distance felt like a knife in the back. And there was no way in hell he was going to say that out loud. "It's not like we were married. For chrissake, Safi. What's going on?"

She stared straight into his eyes until he wanted to look away. "I'm worried about you."

He shook his head, breaking her gaze. "There's nothing to worry about."

"Bullshit. I know you. I thought this job would be good for you. Get your head going in a different direction. But you made a mistake cutting off ties with Manny and Ellie."

"I didn't cut ties. Manny and I will always be friends."

"And Ellie? She was more than a friend. And so is Manny."

Trust Safi to zero in on what he hadn't said. "It was fun, but we all knew it wasn't going to last. It couldn't."

"Yeah, I'm gonna call bullshit again." And she did it so assuredly. "You're deliberately shutting out what could've been the best part of your life. Listen, when Nan and I started dating,

I told myself it would never last. That we were too different, and I'd forget her when we finally decided to go our separate ways. But after two dates, I knew that wasn't going to happen. I knew we'd have a lot of uphill battles because of her background and my need to break everyone who'd hurt her. Makes it difficult to build a relationship with your future in-laws when you want to scream at them for being bigoted assholes."

That made Rob smile, the first true smile in a few days, he realized.

"But I also figured out real quick that I wasn't going to be happy without her in my life so I would have to make some concessions. Like not smashing my fist in her father's face."

And she would've done it. Rob had no doubt about that. When his sister loved you, you either accepted it or you spent the next twenty years learning how avoid her. No one avoided Safi.

"Robbie, sweetheart, you need to get your priorities in order. This job is a great start. It's a challenge and you needed that. But it won't fill your heart."

He wanted to raise his hand and rub it over the abused organ. "My heart's just fine. I don't need a relationship to make me whole."

The look Safi gave him "Not any relationship, no. I just hope when you realize you're wrong, Manny and Ellie will still be around to fill that space."

"I DON'T KNOW about this. What if he really doesn't want to see us? Maybe we should've called ahead."

Manny put his hand on Ellie's nape and squeezed. Her anxiety had manifested in a constant stream of conversation during the drive from Philly to Richmond, where Rob was staying in a hotel near his mom's headquarters until he could find an apartment. She'd talked about everything from her students and her new classes scheduled for the fall to the wildfires in California. He could listen to her recite the alphabet for hours and still have a hard-on.

"Better this way. He can't say no. I talked to Safi and I know where he's staying. She gave me his room number so we can surprise him. I'll text her when we park to see if he's there. She said he's usually back to his room by ten. We should get to the hotel around ten-thirty. We'll surprise him."

"I hope it's not an unwelcome surprise. It feels like we're intruding."

"We're not. Trust me."

"I do trust you."

She smiled up at him and he knew he'd never get enough of her. She was like a drug, one he'd already become addicted to. And didn't want to be cured. Now, they just needed to convince Rob that he was an addict too. And to embrace it.

It only took another couple of minutes to get to the hotel and park in the underground garage. Manny had told her to bring an overnight bag and so had he. Hopefully not wishful thinking.

Once he'd parked, he texted Safi, who told him Rob had left a half hour ago and had said he was going straight home. His mom had a fundraising event tomorrow and Rob needed to be up early to take care of last-minute details. They left the bags in the car and took the elevator to Rob's floor.

Ellie had fallen silent, her hand tight around his as they made their way to his floor. Manny was trying not to show it, but the closer they got to Rob's room, the more tense he became. He didn't want to screw this up. They were at Rob's door before Manny had settled on what exactly he was going to say.

Their pace slowed as they got closer to the door, but Manny hadn't gotten to where he was in life without a backbone.

He knocked on the door and waited, Ellie's hand tightening around his.

No answer. And he didn't hear any movement at all behind the door.

Was he already asleep? Had he gone out? Where the hell—

"Hey."

Rob's voice came from behind them, and they turned, Ellie with a little hitch in her breathing that reminded Manny of how she sounded when he kissed her. He wondered if Rob was thinking the same.

Manny took a good look at his friend, saw the exhaustion, saw the need in his eyes when he looked at Ellie and the welcome when he looked at Manny.

"What are you doing here?"

Manny was about to answer when Ellie beat him to it.

"Well, that's a stupid question." She dropped Manny's hand and walked to Rob. She stopped with only a few inches between them and stuck her right index finger in his chest. "We're here to see you."

Manny's lips twitched at the shock that crossed Rob's face.

"Why haven't you called?"

"I left two days ago. I've been busy."

"Too busy to take two minutes out of your day to let us know how everything is going?"

Rob looked stunned but quickly covered it with indifference as he walked to his door and opened it, waving them through before he followed, shutting it behind them.

"I didn't think you'd care."

"Well, you were wrong." Standing in the middle of the room, Ellie crossed her arms over her chest.

"About what?"

"About thinking you can get away from us that easily."

"I didn't leave you. There was nothing to leave. I took a job."

"Oh, that's bullshit and you know it."

Manny started to grin, which Rob must have seen, because he turned on him with a growl.

"What the hell are you laughing at?"

Manny's grin slid into a smirk. "Did you honestly think you could just walk away and not look back?"

"You don't need me."

The silence stretched for several long seconds until Ellie reached out and smacked her hand against his arm.

"How do you know that?" The look on her face was priceless. Sweet-natured Ellie had become fierce Ellie. Which totally turned Manny on. He loved seeing her like this. And he loved seeing Rob knocked off his axis. "How do you know we don't need you? Why do you think we're here? Did you think we just decided to drive down here for our health?"

Rob was getting frustrated. "Fine. Tell me why you're here."

"Because we *do* need you." She splayed her hand on his chest, looking like a pixie about to square off with a bull. "Even Manny knows that."

She held a hand up in Manny's direction before he could say a word. "I'll get back to you in a second. Right now, Rob needs to know that we didn't drive down here for a quick fuck before we turn around and head back to Philly. We're here because we're willing to give this relationship a chance. Because I believe we can make this work and we're willing to follow you to show you—"

Rob grabbed her upper arms and yanked her against his chest. She gasped just before his mouth descended on hers and he kissed her. For a brief second, Manny wasn't sure she was going to let him shut her down. Her hands were crushed between their bodies, but they were pushing against his chest, as if she wanted to break his hold. But Rob wouldn't let her. He just pulled her in tighter, his head twisting to the side to kiss her deeper.

Manny's cock began to harden. Rob was starved for her, as his almost out-of-control kisses proved. When he released her arms, she wrapped them around his body, squeezing him tight as his hands cupped her face.

But Rob wasn't content to claim her mouth. His hands moved around to her back and splayed across it, pressing her closer. She snuggled closer without hesitation, her hips arching into his body, urging him to take more. To give her more.

Manny's cock throbbed as he watched Rob devour her. He wondered what Rob would do if Manny walked over and started to strip her?

An unfamiliar uncertainty held his feet to the floor. He wanted to give Rob and Ellie space, but he wanted to move their relationship to the next level. He just wasn't sure Rob was ready.

He got the answer to his unspoken question when Rob released her mouth and looked over her head, directly at Manny. In his eyes, Manny saw an apology and an invitation. Which he wasn't going to ignore.

Manny closed the distance between them, stopping just shy of being pressed up against Ellie. She turned her head to look over her shoulder at him, and he bent to press his lips to her cheek. When he drew back, Rob grabbed her shirt and pulled it over her head. She wore a simple cotton skirt and top, the blue of the top matching her eyes perfectly. She looked beautiful in it. She looked stunning out of it.

Especially when Manny tugged the skirt off her hips and let it fall to the floor. Now she wore only matching bra and panties of the palest pink that made him want to fall to his knees and worship her with his mouth.

Rob beat him to it. He was on his knees, his lips pressing against the soft skin of her belly just above the waistline of her panties. Ellie gasped, her hands braced on his shoulders and her body swaying.

Manny closed the few inches between them, his front pressed against her almost bare back. The heat of her skin burned through the thin material of his t-shirt. Reaching behind his head, he pulled his shirt off and groaned as he soaked her in just before he bent his head. He reached for her jaw and turned her head so he could reach her mouth. The throaty sigh she made reached inside his chest and squeezed his heart in a vise.

A second later, her entire body tightened. Manny opened his eyes to see Rob part her thighs and put his mouth and his tongue to work between her legs. Ellie's one hand rose to clasp Manny's nape while the other gripped Rob's shoulder.

A heartbeat later, Manny felt her surrender in the shudder that ran through her body.

And he smiled.

ROB FELT Ellie shudder and grinned, because he knew she'd just given herself over to them. Not that he'd had any doubt when she'd stuck that finger in his chest and declared that they were there for him and he would get on board or else.

He hadn't known he needed to hear it until the words had come out of her mouth. Now he needed to assure her that he was on board. He and Manny would make sure she never doubted their dedication to her. If it took months or years, it wouldn't matter. They'd still be here.

Here was a really good place to be. With his tongue sliding between the slick folds of her sex and his hands on her thighs keeping them open so he could make her come.

While Manny kept her mouth occupied, his tongue found her clit, playing with it until she started to squirm. Alternating between a light flick and a firm swipe, he pushed her toward a quick orgasm. The first of what would be several tonight. He'd make damn sure of it.

His hands slid around her thighs to squeeze the firm globes of her ass, the softness of her skin its own sweet pleasure. She shook, her muscles quivering, the hand on his shoulder tightening. They wouldn't let her fall, not with Manny propping her up from behind and Rob supporting her from the front.

But he wanted her to let go. He concentrated on listening to what her body was telling him, how she sucked in a sharp breath when his teeth grazed her clit, and how she sighed and arched closer when he used just the tip of his tongue to tease her pussy lips.

When her movements became more frantic, he knew he had her where he wanted her. Without warning, he speared two fingers into her channel at the same time he sucked on her clit.

She came with a deep groan, slightly muffled by Manny's mouth on hers. She wanted to move but they had her wrapped in their arms so tightly, she could only shake with the strength of her climax.

While she was still wracked by the aftermath, Rob stood, his gaze meeting Manny's, who continued to hold her upright with his arms around her waist and shoulders.

"Let's take this to the bed."

Manny's grin was all teeth as he scooped Ellie into his arms, then waited for Rob to get up off his knees before leading them to the separate bedroom in the rear of the suite.

Rob didn't turn on any lights in the bedroom. There was more than enough ambient light from the living area for him to see as he walked to the bed and stripped the cover down to the foot of the bed. He stripped out of his loose cotton pants, leaving him naked. And ready. God damn, he was ready.

Taking Ellie from Manny, he laid her out on the bed and followed her down, while Manny stripped out of his clothes. Rolling onto his side, Rob put her between them, as Manny set a bottle of lube he must've had in his pocket on the side table.

Glancing at the bottle then at Manny, Ellie smiled. She knew what Manny wanted. What Rob wanted. What she was going to get.

She held out her hand to Manny, who came down next to her and took her mouth, kissing her as he swept a hand down her body to her thighs. She parted her legs, expecting him to go straight for her pussy. Instead, he stroked her inner thighs, making her sigh and her body practically melt into the bed. Rob watched, his desire for her coiling into a red-hot ball in his gut. After several long minutes, Manny stopped petting her and abruptly turned her on her side toward Rob.

Her arms curved around Rob's shoulders, and she kissed him as her body molded against the length of his. His aching cock nestled against her stomach, the soft flesh warm against his heated shaft. His hands grabbed her hips and pulled her even closer, content to rub his cock against her for now. But that's not what she wanted.

Rolling on top of him, she straddled Rob's hips, her hands planted on his chest to hold herself upright. With her gaze locked on his, she rubbed her pussy against his shaft, teasing him, until he grabbed her hips and took over the rhythm. Her eyes closed as she gave him control until she froze when Manny positioned himself behind her, one hand on her shoulder, the other cupping the back of her head and gently pushing her forward.

Rob took that moment to slide her hips up so his cock could slip between her folds and press against her entrance. He slipped inside her, just the tip, and held, the temptation to pump into her a ruthless need he barely controlled. But he knew what Manny was planning so he held still, even as Ellie tried to take him deeper.

She froze when Manny slicked his fingers between her ass cheeks. A drop of the lube on his fingers fell onto Rob's cock and slipped down to his balls, making his control waver. Then she blew it to hell when she wiggled her hips and took him in almost completely.

He arched, seating himself deep.

"Manny, hurry the fuck up."

Manny's hand pressed her head into Rob's shoulder then stroked down her back, as Rob swept his hands up her sides then wrapped his arms around her upper body, holding her tight.

"Let me know if it's too much." Manny's voice sounded like a growl and Ellie shuddered and clenched around Rob, making him groan.

"Just do it already. I'm—"

Manny started to push inside, tightening her pussy around Rob as Manny forged inside her ass. He went so slow, Rob wasn't sure he was going to be able to wait for Manny to get all the way inside. But neither of them wanted to hurt Ellie.

Rob felt her labored breathing against his neck, but before he felt her bite his collarbone. The eroticism of the moment hit every one of Rob's triggers, and he felt his body begin to spiral out of his control.

And when Manny finally had his cock buried deep in Ellie's ass, Rob gave up on control and let instinct take over.

Rob pulled out slowly as Manny held still, both of them wary of hurting her. But Ellie had plans of her own. And though Manny and Rob might think they were strong enough to withstand her desires, they were fast learning that wasn't an option.

Every little move, every tiny contraction of her body made them respond. When her pussy clenched around Rob, he had to move. Which made Manny move, as well.

They found a rhythm, thrust and retreat, torturing all three of them. Ellie couldn't move much, but when she managed, he and Manny danced to her tune.

And it was a dance. A wild one that left all three of them on an edge so sharp, it felt dangerous.

Rob felt his release building way faster than he wanted but he knew he wasn't going to be able to stop it, not this time. And when he looked up at Manny, his eyes closed and his mouth drawn tight, he could tell his friend was there with him.

And when Ellie gasped, her body tightening around them and making them groan in unison, Rob gave in.

Arching his hips, he pumped deep and came, Ellie on his heels. Seconds later, he felt the pulse of Manny's release, and Ellie's moan in response.

And he knew this was the adventure his life had been missing.

"ARE you really sure this is what you want?"

Still trying to catch her breath, Ellie snuggled against Manny's side, Rob's body a furnace at her back. Rob's question took a few seconds to cycle through her brain before she realized what he was asking.

"Ask me that question when I'm not absolutely wrecked from an amazing orgasm."

Manny's snort of laughter made her feel all gooey inside, but the pinch Rob gave to her ass make her jump, even as she started to laugh.

"Ellie. I'm serious."

Yes, he was. She heard it in his voice. "And trust me when I say, so am I."

"This won't be easy." Rob threaded the fingers of one hand through her hair and gave a gentle tug, his other hand petting her thigh. "People are going to talk."

Maneuvering onto her stomach between them, her upper body propped up on her elbows, she looked first at Rob, then at Manny. Manny's eyes had been closed until a second ago, but now he turned to look at Rob.

Their gazes caught and held, and Ellie knew Manny saw the hesitation in Rob's gaze, just as she did. She wanted to erase that doubt, wanted him to take the same leap she and Manny were prepared to do.

"Let them talk." Manny's response was way more succinct than she would've been. "Dude, you jump off mountains for the thrill. This is the adventure of a lifetime."

Rob didn't respond, but she saw the moment he made up his mind to take the leap. He reached for her, pulling her up onto his chest, and looking into her eyes.

"And I'm in it to the end."

BE sure to check out Brianna's story in Sharing Brianna, coming soon...

The Instigator

The Playboy

The D-Man

The Machine

FAST ICE

Bylines & Blue Lines

Hard Lines & Goal Lines

Deadlines & Red Lines

MOONLIGHT LOVERS

Kiss of Moonlight

Visions in Moonlight

Edge of Moonlight

Temptation in Moonlight

Grace in Moonlight

Shades of Moonlight

MAGICAL SEDUCTION

Seduced by Magic

Seduced in Shadow

Seduced & Ensnared

Seduced & Enchanted

Seduced by Chaos

Seduced by Danger

Moonlight Seduction

FORGOTTEN GODDESSES

ABOUT THE AUTHOR

Stephanie Julian is a USA Today and New York Times best-selling author of contemporary and paranormal romance. Make sure you sign up to receive all of her news at www.stephaniejulian.com.